P9-DER-672

Imago Bird

By the same author

Spaces of the Dark
The Rainbearers
Corruption
Meeting Place
Accident
Assassins
Impossible Object
Natalie Natalia
Catastrophe Practice
Serpent
Judith

African Switchback
The Life of Raymond Raynes
Experience and Religion
The Assassination of Trotsky
Julian Grenfell
Rules of the Game: Sir Oswald and Lady Cynthia Mosley
    1896-1933
Beyond the Pale: Sir Oswald Mosley 1933-1980

Imago Bird

Nicholas Mosley

The Dalkey Archive Press

Originally published by Martin Secker & Warburg Ltd., England, 1980
Copyright © 1980 Nicholas Mosley
Revised edition copyright © 1989 Nicholas Mosley
All rights reserved

Library of Congress Cataloging in Publication Data
Mosley, Nicholas, 1923-
    Imago Bird / Nicholas Mosley. — 1st American ed.
    I. Title.
PR6063.082I44   1989   823'.914—dc19   88-30392
ISBN: 0-916583-36-8

First American Edition

Partially funded by grants from The National Endowment for the Arts and
The Illinois Arts Council.

The Dalkey Archive Press
1817 North 79th Avenue
Elmwood Park, IL 60635 USA

IMAGO . . . . 1. Final and perfect stage of an insect after it has undergone its metamorphosis, e.g., butterfly.

2. Idealised mental picture of oneself or another person, especially parent.

I

Ever since I can remember I have thought the grown-up world to be mad; its way of talking to itself and being outraged at the answers; the bright look in its eye as it goes off to feed on disaster. Aristotle said it was self-evident that human beings wanted happiness; but it seems to me they are more at home in sadness and confusion; that if these are taken away they are exposed to the heat of the sun like snails without shells or dark places.

When I was eighteen I was staying with my uncle who happened at the time to be Prime Minister. He was not living at 10 Downing Street because, I think, he did not expect to be Prime Minister for long. He lived in the house in Cowley Street where he had been when he was Leader of the Opposition. I was staying with Uncle Bill because my mother and father were abroad – my father was working on a film in India and my mother was involved in social work in California – and it had been arranged before Uncle Bill became Prime Minister that I should stay at his house in London and should go each day to see a doctor. It was thought I should go to a doctor because I stammered. I had stammered quite badly since I was seven. My stammer played a great and terrible part in my life, yet I seemed oddly reluctant to try to get rid of it. I sometimes wondered if in this respect I were representative of what I felt about the grown-up world.

At the time at which I am beginning this story (why do people write stories? in the hope they might not be talking to themselves?) I had been going to this doctor for an hour each weekday. Where Dr Anders lived was an hour's journey from Cowley Street, by underground and on foot, so my visits took up most of the afternoons. I spent most of these mornings in bed. I had done my A levels at school that summer, and I had a year to wait before going to a university. I would lie in my room at the top of Uncle Bill's house and would listen for footsteps coming up the stairs. I both was sad that people did not more often come to visit me, and planned how I might hide from them if they did.

I had been to two or three other doctors before about my stammer. One of these had said, after months — Perhaps you don't want to get rid of your stammer. I had been outraged by this. I had also thought — Isn't it your job to make me want to get rid of my stammer?

My room in Uncle Bill's house was next door to the attic. Once or twice during these mornings Uncle Bill came up to see me. He would stand at the bottom of my bed looking huge beneath the Dr Caligari ceilings, while I pretended I had been sitting up for some time working. He asked me if I would not like to decorate my room — to stick posters and suchlike on the walls — to make myself feel more at home there. I thought I might explain that I did not want to feel at home there: that I wanted home to be somewhere in my head, where I might one day get to. But I thought this would sound ungrateful, and pretentious.

When I had first gone to Dr Anders, just before the time when I am beginning this story, I had told her of what the previous therapist had said about my possibly not wanting to get rid of my stammer; and she had said, cheerfully — But of course you don't want to get rid of your stammer! And I had felt for a moment that I should be outraged again at this; and then I had felt as if I were starting on some journey.

I should have explained that Dr Anders is a woman. She has a brown wrinkled face, blue eyes, and a pudding-basin haircut. When I talked to her this first time there was the impression that the journey we were embarking on was one of which she had had a sudden glimpse of the end, and it was this that made her cheerful.

I had from time to time realised that my stammer might be some protection.

On the day when I am beginning this story Uncle Bill had been having a row with his secretary, Mrs Washbourne. He and Mrs Washbourne often had these rows: I think they gave to them some sense of protection; of being at home in an irrational world that they felt they had to try to order. I had been coming down the stairs at Cowley Street into the hall when I heard Uncle Bill shouting from behind the closed door of his study. Noises in this household often seemed to come from behind closed doors: it was as if we were from time to time involved in some Greek tragedy. Uncle Bill used to shout at Mrs Washbourne in a quite impersonal way as if he were selling newspapers; or as if he were the man in Greek tragedy who specialised in making noises of murder or self-mutilation off-stage. And Mrs Washbourne would smile rather knowingly as if she were the Mona Lisa with a moustache drawn on her. Of course I could not see Mrs Washbourne through the closed door of the study, but this was a scene that had been enacted often enough before to have created some sort of pattern.

I do not know how I should try to describe these people. Novelists I suppose try to make their characters life-like; but also for propriety they try to disguise them. However most people, and especially politicians, seem to spend much of their lives pretending to be someone else: so perhaps it is life-like to make Uncle Bill and Mrs Washbourne, who were having an affair, to appear somewhat like actors.

Uncle Bill was a large red-faced man with white hair. Mrs Washbourne had gold hair and was rather icy. After a time of shouting, Uncle Bill would take his spectacles off his nose and hold them by his groin and whirl them round and round there as if they were catherine wheels and he was signalling some sort of relief or celebration.

On the evening of this particular row I was standing on the stairs and listening to the noises from behind closed doors (why did the Greeks make things like murder and self-mutilation happen off-stage? was it because they knew that these things are mostly in the imagination?) when Aunt Mavis — I have not before mentioned Aunt Mavis: people often seem not quite to mention Aunt Mavis: as if she were a member of the chorus of a Greek tragedy, there only to carry reflections of the terrible events off-stage — when Aunt Mavis came from the dining-room into the hall. She was carrying a glass. When people do not mention Aunt Mavis perhaps it is because she often, at that time, seemed to be carrying a glass. She is a thin, rather concave woman as if people had been treading too much on her and she has become hollowed out like a step. When she heard Uncle Bill shouting she stood still. She looked up at me on the stairs; or rather she seemed to look right through me — as though I were a member of an audience and thus in a different category to that of the people on a stage.

I wondered — Did the Greeks like to be told of murder and self-mutilation off-stage because this reassured them that other people had awful imaginations like their own? But nowadays people want their stage-horrors in full view, so this could mean they might begin to think their imaginations funny —

Aunt Mavis stood in the hall with her drink in her hand. She looked right through me. I thought — Might not actors in fact begin to glimpse their audience as if it were their unconscious? Then Uncle Bill stopped shouting; and there would be Mrs Washbourne looking at him with her smile drawn on her like a rope; tugging at him with it, or at his spectacles, as if they were rings through a bull's testicles —

There was a silence in the hall for a time. Then there was the sound of a pistol shot.

Or perhaps I thought it was like a pistol shot because that was the sort of thing we had come to expect from behind closed doors.

What had Uncle Bill and Mrs Washbourne been doing, we as an audience might ask, in those moments before the pistol shot? Had she taken out a pistol to stop him shouting? Had he taken out a pistol to stop her smile? I had thought it suited Uncle Bill and Mrs Washbourne to be thus shouting and smiling. How else could people like King Agamemnon and Queen Clytemnestra, who were otherwise so boring, gain an audience's attention? And they could come alive again, of course, after a pistol shot: to be ready for the next night's murder and self-mutilation.

Uncle Bill came out of his study. He was this red-faced man

with white hair. He was carrying his spectacles by his groin. He said 'I was cleaning it.' Aunt Mavis said 'Was it dirty?' I was much interested at that time, since I was going to Dr Anders, in psychoanalytic language; which of course is supposed to point out the connections between things like pistols and penises. Aunt Mavis was leaning towards Uncle Bill with her glass in her hand, as if she were a bull and he were her matador. He said 'Is that funny?' She said 'Is it meant to be?' There was the peculiar tension between them which actors can create just by doing nothing on stage. Uncle Bill said 'It hit the ceiling.' Aunt Mavis said 'That's where you were aiming it?' I did think this quite funny. It seemed as if they had forgotten their lines and were ad-libbing; or were waiting for the prompter to say something off-stage. Then Uncle Bill looked at me. I thought I should try and say something, since otherwise he might notice that I had thought this funny. When I begin to stammer it is as if a valve gets stuck in my head and I go on breathing in and cannot breathe out; I become like a diver with a madman at my wind-pipe. I was trying to say two things at once: both — I came downstairs to ask what I should wear tomorrow night (I was being taken to some party the following night); also — It's all right, I won't tell anyone. Because of course there would be people interested in things like pistol shots between Uncle Bill and Mrs Washbourne, even if he had just been cleaning a pistol which I suppose he might have been however unlikely this was according to psychoanalytic language. I had heard a rumour that Government Ministers had recently been allowed to keep pistols, after the kidnap and murder of some Italian politician when his body-guard had been shot; and it seemed probable that Uncle Bill might like possessing a pistol. But he and Mrs Washbourne would not in any case want anyone to know about a shot: so it looked as if I had them in some sort of power. But I did not want to have them in any power, at least not in this sort which was trivial. Stammering, it seems to me, is often caused by a person's wanting to say two or more things at once; which, it also seems, is often the only way in which things can be made to sound true. But ordinary language is not suited to this: or at least, not without the struggle.

5

Mrs Washbourne came out of the study into the hall. She was this statuesque woman with gold hair. She was holding her left wrist with her right hand. I wondered if Uncle Bill had shot her there. She was wearing a dress with wide flat shoulders so that she looked like the Jack of Clubs. The Jack of Clubs is one with fair hair but no moustache. I thought — Or Uncle Bill might have shot her smile off? She said 'I just think he should see someone that's all.' Aunt Mavis said 'See who?' Mrs Washbourne said 'See anyone.' They were talking about Uncle Bill as if he were not there. I remembered this sort of scene from my childhood — an aunt and my mother talking in front of me as if I were not there. (I thought — Or as if I were their unconscience?) Uncle Bill said 'Where's Woodcock?' Woodcock was one of the detectives put on to guard Uncle Bill. We seemed to be waiting for Woodcock to come in like the prompter; or like a stage-manager from another dimension to tell us that the murders and self-mutilations were not real.

After a time Woodcock did come in. He was a man without striking features — the ten of clubs, perhaps, after the King and Queen and Jack. Mrs Washbourne said 'Can't he say he did it?' Aunt Mavis said 'Can't he say he did what?' Mrs Washbourne said 'I suppose he'd lose his job.' They were still talking as if neither Uncle Bill nor Woodcock were there. Woodcock went through into the study. I could see him looking up at the ceiling and then at the walls and the floor. Aunt Mavis said 'He shouldn't have been playing with it.' Mrs Washbourne said 'Why do you think he was playing with it?' I wondered how much any of them knew about psychoanalytic language. Aunt Mavis began to smile. When Aunt Mavis smiles, she seems at the same time to be trying to keep her mouth straight, as if it were a mountain-ledge from which she is hanging. I was still trying to get more breath in, or out, or anything: I was like a balloon over a volcano. Uncle Bill said 'Have you seen a vision or something?' He was talking to me. It was unusual, in front of others, for him to talk to me. What he had said was a reference, I think, to something I had once told him, which was that I had bicycled to Bognor one day to visit the beach where Blake had seen visions: I had collected some shells there. I had at last to let my breath out: at the end was a small hiccup, like a pendant. I thought that now I might smile. Uncle Bill was smiling. I thought — But do not Japanese people smile when things are alarming? Mrs Washbourne said 'You frighten me.' Aunt Mavis said 'You frighten me too.' Woodcock came back into the hall. It was as if he were a person who has found what he has been looking for in a game of hunt-the-thimble. He locked the door of the study behind him. Aunt Mavis began coming towards me on the stairs. Sometimes when Aunt Mavis comes towards you she seems about to go, as well as to look, right through you; but even for ghosts you have to step aside. I thought — Actors have that smile on their faces like mad archaic statues: they are trying to get back to an impossibly innocent past. By this time other secretaries and aides had come into the hall. I thought — Soon there will be enough for a full crowd-scene; then we can jump up and down and shout things like Rhubarb rhubarb; and we will not have to worry any more about meanings. Woodcock was putting the key of the study door into his pocket. I thought — But if what happens off-stage really goes on in the mind, then indeed can it not be seen as funny? even murder and self-mutilation? And might not this, the knowledge of it, stop it? However — What about language then, for protection and self-justification. The people who had come into the hall were not quite looking at Uncle Bill; nor at Mrs Washbourne; not quite catching each other's eyes. I thought — Actors of course do not recognise each other as they really are when they are on the stage: it is their job to pretend, to cover up, to put something over. And by this they give comfort. The people in the hall were already not interested in finding out what in fact had happened in the study: they were interested in discovering what sort of parts they should play in order to preserve, whatever had happened, some customary function and identity. Like this they could give comfort: but did not the reality, locked in the study, remain in their unconscious like a hungry lion?

II

'There was a shot — '

'Yes.'

'And your uncle came out of his room — '

'Yes.'

'And said — I was cleaning it — '

One thing that happens in the course of analysis is that you are made to feel something of a fool. Or rather, you feel as if you would have been made to feel a fool if you had been talking to anyone but your analyst. But because one of the reasons that you have gone to him or her is that you think he or she might know more about what you are trying to say than you do yourself, so, on this quite different level — that of learning — you do not feel a fool at all.

I said '— Why shouldn't he have been cleaning a pistol — ?'

Dr Anders said 'You think he might not have been?'

I said 'You mean — What would he have been cleaning a pistol for, while he was shouting at Mrs Washbourne — ?'

What analysts do is to get you to play your words back to yourself so it is as if you can hear yourself speaking. Then you begin to question yourself, because you hear different patterns and inflexions. It is like hearing your voice on tape; but the difference from what you expected is not just of tone, but of content and intention.

Dr Anders said 'You knew he had this pistol — '

I said 'I knew there was a rumour that people like him could have pistols — '

'Well if it went off he must have got it.'

It is a layman's idea about analysts I suppose that they take ordinary words and ideas and translate them into things like breasts and penises. And often they do. But they do not like it if you suggest this.

I said 'Why am I smiling — ?'

She said 'Well, why are you?'

I thought — But it is another of the jobs of analysts after all to encourage you not to mind too much if other people do not like it when you suggest things.

Dr Anders said 'Do you really think it is myself who, when you say something like pistols, makes you make the connection between them and penises?'

I wanted to say — Well, don't you?

I said 'Well I think it's under your influence that I do.'

She said 'Why?'

I wanted to say — Because it's funny.

Or — Aren't you trying to make me see that whatever connections are already there, are funny?

I said 'Well, it's funny.'

She said 'You haven't told me much about it yet.'

Sometimes with Dr Anders there was a warm and pleasant feeling as if you were lying in a bedroom with a fire in the dark.

I looked at her bookcase, the frieze on her wall, the spire beyond her window.

I said 'Well, I was coming down the stairs and Aunt Mavis was coming out of the dining-room. Then there was this shot. I'm sure it was a shot. Then Uncle Bill came out of the study. But what actually happened inside, of course, I have absolutely no means of knowing.'

'Why not?'

'How could I?'

'You could have asked.'

'Who? When?'

I thought — Can I not say, I would have stammered?

Then — But this is what she expects me to say: which will prove that I use my stammer as some sort of protection?

I said ' — Ask Uncle Bill if he'd taken a pot shot at Mrs Washbourne — ?'

I thought I should explain — Anyway, none of this is what matters: the point is the way in which we were all there like people in a theatre; in which neither actors nor audience in fact do ask what is going on behind the stage.

9

Sometimes with Dr Anders it was as if so many things were coming into my head at once that it was like all the lights coming on in the auditorium.

I said 'But the odd thing was that what had really happened didn't seem to be of importance: we were all just standing around waiting for the cover-up to begin: as if this were the whole purpose of people being involved in the drama.'

She said 'A mystery drama.'

I said 'Yes.'

Then — 'If you like.'

One of the patterns that seemed to be emerging from my sessions with Dr Anders was the way in which she claimed to have spotted in me a liking for turning things into mysteries; while I claimed that it was life itself that consisted of mysteries, which I tried to observe truly but which other people always seemed to be trying to turn into simple dramas that were false.

And in fact, did I not see myself as someone who was asking what was going on behind the stage?

I said 'It's their mystery. They won't want to solve it. They'll chew it over for weeks. How else would they pass their time?'

Dr Anders said nothing.

Sometimes when Dr Anders said nothing I knew she did not approve of what I was saying: but because I knew she wanted me to learn not to mind too much whether or not she approved, I both did and did not mind this.

I said 'What on earth can politicians do? They have to make up mysteries, hostilities, dramas: who has shot at whom: how the bridesmaids have behaved. What else is their life? Of course, sometimes, something has happened. But still, they would see their job as the cover-up; the story; the question of advantage; not what really had happened.'

Dr Anders used to sit in profile to where I lay. When I first had come to Dr Anders and had had to lie on her awful couch I had wondered whether or not I should take off my shoes. I had thought — If I do she will think I am overscrupulous; if I do not she will think I am dirty.

I said now — 'I suppose I could have gone into the study and looked at the ceiling.'

She said 'Yes.'

I said 'He did seem to say there was a hole there.'

I thought I might add — You see why I'm smiling?

Dr Anders' brown wrinkled face is like a nut that might sprout after millions of years.

She said 'But what you said you found yourself actually thinking was — Now I've got you!'

I said 'But also I said, I didn't want this.'

She said 'So that's why things seem mysteries?'

Sometimes in analysis such a bright light comes down that it is like a curtain in front of the stage and all the audience seems to be leaving the theatre.

I thought — So what is it now from which I am trying to protect myself?

There was Dr Anders' bookcase, her frieze, the spire beyond her window.

When I had gone for my initial interview with Dr Anders I had not then lain down on her couch but had sat in a chair opposite her: and when she had said — But of course you don't want to get rid of your stammer! — and I had been so outraged at this but had also thought — Well, all right, we are off on our long journey — I had kept wondering about this as the interview went on: and towards the end I had said — Why, if it is such hell, do I not want to get rid of my stammer? And she had said — You think people want to get out of hell? And this had been the first time that I felt the light that was like the glow of a fire in a bedroom somewhere beside me: and it was this that was like the beginning of a journey; and also the glimpse of the end of it. For although I knew that I myself thought things like this — about hell being something that people did not want to get out of — I did not know that other people thought this; and this knowing was some liberation. So I had said — But if I do not want to get out of hell because hell is a protection, what is it that I am using my stammer as a protection against? And I had thought she might say, as one of my earlier therapists had once said — Might not you be using your stammer as a protection against other people's disapproval? or against your own anger? And I had never quite thought this sufficiently subtle. So when

I had put this question to Dr Anders and she had not answered for a time I had felt — Well, I suppose your answer will be the same as other people's: and then she had said — Might you not be using your stammer as a protection against your own high opinion of yourself?

There was the white light like something fusing: then her bookcase, her frieze, the spire beyond her window.

I thought — If one jumped, might one not fly?

She said 'Of what are you thinking?'

I said 'Of the first time I came to see you.'

She said 'What about it?'

I said 'You said what I might be protecting myself against was my own high opinion of myself.'

She said nothing.

When I had first come for proper sessions with her and had had to lie down, I had taken my shoes off. Then I had thought — Would I not have learned more if she had seen me as dirty?

I said 'But I couldn't ask there and then, in the hall, what had happened in the study. It would have been rude. And anyway, I did just stammer.'

She said 'What were you trying to say when you stammered?'

I said 'I was going to ask whether I should get some new clothes for this party they're taking me to tonight: also I was trying to say — Don't worry, I won't say anything.'

'About the pistol shot — '

'Yes.'

I thought — What was that image that came into my mind a moment ago when I was thinking my mind was a blank and I was looking through the window?

She said 'That was when you felt — Now I've got you!'

'Well — '

'A feeling of triumph — '

'But also not.'

— There are birds that sometimes perch on that ledge beyond the window — ?

Then — But there is no reason why I should not have a feeling of power? And so I stammer?

I felt a sudden cold run up and down my spine, as if there

were Gadarene swine rushing there.

I said 'I see.'

She said 'What do you see?'

— A window-ledge; a courtyard; a drop on to some railings — I said 'If the story got out, I suppose it would damage him.'

She said nothing.

I said 'Do you mean, if I had managed to ask exactly what had happened, I might not have stammered?'

She had a way of pursing her lips as if by this she were getting hand-hold on a mountain.

I thought — But is it a good or bad protection then that I stammer?

— For I do not, do I, really want to hurt them —

When the lights come on so brightly in the theatre of your mind it is as if you were in a maze in which you have been travelling and have lost your way; you stand between green walls and look for a thread which was spun by some loved one years ago.

I said 'But that's what I hate about the grown-up world, they talk so fluently, whether they're telling stories, or stories to cover up stories, they're still not trying to find out how things are. Language isn't suited to finding out this: language is for arguing, attacking, getting protection, getting responses. Stammering is perhaps a sign of trying to find out how things are: things are so complicated: there are so many of them: you can't get near them without a struggle.'

Dr Anders said 'Lucky old you.'

I thought I might make a noise as if I were someone behind a closed door and being murdered.

Then — Do other people think me lucky then?

If you stand in the maze long enough, what seems to happen is that the walls begin to shake and holes to appear as if you are in some sort of sieve.

I said 'What probably happened was that Uncle Bill had just been mucking about with this gun and then it went off. I expect he does like guns. He's often shouting at Mrs Washbourne. God knows what connections there are in anyone's unconscious, or conscious.'

Dr Anders said nothing.

I said 'I had an image just now — '

Then — I might have wanted to destroy them?

I said 'No, it's gone.'

There was Dr Anders' bookcase, her frieze, the spire beyond her window.

I said 'So they make up stories — '

— A pond with a duck on it —

I said 'Oh I know I make up stories too! Perhaps I do like mysteries. Then I can feel — what — I told you so! Then I do feel superior. Yes. But I know it and they don't. And still, I don't really like it. That's the difference. That's what I hate, their all being on a stage and acting so sincerely. As if they believed in their dramas. What does it matter if a pistol does go off? They treat life like a detective story.'

Dr Anders said 'But the point of a detective story is to find out exactly what happened.'

I said 'But in fact it's just a man with a blank cartridge behind the stage.'

Dr Anders said nothing.

I said 'The whole play, or story, is just a pretence to amuse an audience.'

Dr Anders seemed to be considering something quite different.

I thought — But have I not, for the last ten minutes, been amusing?

Perhaps I could explain — Might I not be both actor, and audience, in my own drama —

Or I could cry out — Is not the thread through the maze the cold air through the holes which appear when the walls begin to shake and come down —

Dr Anders said 'Do you know, for the last ten minutes, you haven't been stammering?'

I said 'Haven't I?'

I thought — Or something wrapped like a cocoon or a baby in front of the fire —

Dr Anders said 'I'm not saying it would be easy.'

I said 'What would not be easy?'

Then — ' — Not easy to find out exactly what's happening — ?'

Dr Anders leaned forward and raised her hands slightly from the arms of her chair. This was her signal that we were coming to the end of the session. It was also the signal, sometimes, for a rush of thoughts and images to come into my head as if they had been waiting just for this to be like children let out of school.

I said 'But if my stammer is a protection against my destructive feelings, should I or should I not stammer?'

Dr Anders remained leaning forward with her hands on the arms of her chair.

I said ' — I haven't stammered for ten minutes because I've been contemptuous and trivial and aggressive — ?'

She said 'Yes, that's a problem.'

She still did not quite get up from her chair.

I said 'The more you find out, the more you find what's impossible. Neuroses are like shells: you lose them and you burn up in the sun. But if you don't lose them, they grow so heavy you go mad too.'

Dr Anders got up from her chair. She went to the door slowly. She sometimes held her leg as if she had been kicked by a horse there.

I said 'So isn't it better to be gentle and helpless than to pour out your shit?'

I thought — And I'm still not stammering — ?

She turned with her hand on the handle of the door. She said 'You think you can choose?'

III

I had a girlfriend at the time called Sheila who lived near Belsize Park. This was within walking distance from Dr Anders'. I used to visit Sheila in the afternoons after I had been to Dr Anders. Like this I did not have to telephone to make arrangements. I hate telephoning: and to make arrangements seems to me to be presumptuous in a world where anything may turn up.

Sheila said 'Was there a lock on the front door when you came in?'

I said 'Why, has someone stolen it?'

Sheila lived in a house with a lot of squatters and tenants who did not pay much rent because the ground-lease was nearly up and the landlord was doing nothing about renovations. Sheila was one of a group of Young Trotskyites. I liked the fact that Sheila was a Trotskyite; not, I think, because I found it easier to be committed to her sort of politics than to Uncle Bill's, but because I felt there was something interesting in moving between the two.

Sheila said 'What did the old witch get out of you today?'

I said 'Not much.'

She said 'Just breasts and cunts and penises.'

Sheila was a big, round-faced girl with short hair. She had a skin which was rather like ice before you skate on it. She wore very tight trousers; in which she seemed to hang like things in a larder.

I said 'And little bits of shit which, when I was young, were rejected by an unappreciative world.'

She said 'I do think that's all balls.'

I said 'And crap — '

'And crap — '

'And shit — '

Sheila's room had two old frames containing bedsprings on the floor, and a lot of cushions. There were some bits of seaweed and driftwood on the walls which she and I had collected from the beach near Bognor where Blake had seen visions.

She said 'That's how we're conditioned to talk. By people like you and your fucking analyst. You don't think people would talk like this naturally, do you?'

Sheila was a few years older than I. She was doing social science at London University. She felt rather belligerent about doing social science, because so many Young Trotskyites were doing it.

I said 'How do you think the workers will talk after the revolution? — Will you please pass the cucumber sandwiches — ?'

Sheila said ' — Will you pass you and your uncle's head on a fucking platter — '

Sheila and I used to talk like this I suppose because we were not in love. People talked like this on television and in films. I thought — It is this that is our conditioning.

I said 'What's the matter with you today, have you been tortured by the police?'

Sheila began to take off her clothes. She had difficulty in getting her trousers off, as if they were sails in a high wind.

It was accepted that Sheila and I made love in the afternoons. It was useful to me that this was accepted, because then I did not have to go through the preliminary moves and stages which I was not good at.

She said 'And what's been going on in your grand world? Have you met any particularly loathsome specimens lately?'

I said 'I'm going to this reception tonight. For this Asian or African Prime Minister.'

She said 'Which Asian or African Prime Minister?'

I thought I might say — They all look alike to me. But I wondered — What would I be protecting myself against by making jokes that I do not mean?

Also I sometimes imagined Sheila might in fact have a tape-recorder in her room, to take down my words and use them one day against me.

I said 'Mr Perhaia.'

'Who's Mr Perhaia?'

I said 'I thought you knew about such things.'

When Sheila finally did get her trousers off she stood like the figurehead of a ship with her arms by her side and her lower half blown by spray. I took my clothes off.

She said 'God you take it for granted don't you.'

I said 'Well you do too.'

'How did you get it up the stairs?'

'I used it to knock the lock off.'

'That's how you describe it is it.'

'As if this house ever had any locks!'

'You'd like that wouldn't you?'

'What — '

'I'll show you.'

Although it was accepted that Sheila and I made love in the afternoons, and I liked this, it sometimes seemed difficult to turn into reality what my mind told me I so much desired.

She said 'What's wrong?'

'Nothing.'

'You were all right a moment ago.'

'And now I'm not.'

I do not know what other people find about these things. People seldom tell the truth about making love. What I used to find was that although of course I looked forward to it very much, and it was of course very good when it happened, there was a moment in between when sometimes things went blank as if there were the lights coming on in the auditorium or the thread had got lost in the maze.

She said 'Is it something to do with me?'

'No.'

'What is it then?'

'Wait.'

I had asked Dr Anders if other people found anything like this. She had said — as she usually said to such questions — Why are you interested in what other people find?

I wondered — Would it be different if we were in love?

— Or if we did not take it so much for granted —

Also — Are these things the same then —

Sheila said 'Was it because of what I said about you and your uncle's head on a platter?'

'No.'

'What was it then?'

I thought — But in love you would take both everything and nothing for granted —

When I had first been with Sheila this sudden failure had been terrible. Then, when things had worked out all right once or twice, it was not too oppressive.

Sheila said 'You don't really think, do you, when I ask you questions about your grand world, I'm trying to get something out of you?'

I said 'No.'

'Because if you do, it's pathetic!'

When Sheila flung herself back on the bedsprings they would rock her up and down gently for a time like a boat.

I thought — Is it true then that she might be trying to get something out of me?

But also — It is when we act as if we are angry that things get better.

I did have this fantasy about Sheila perhaps using me to find out things about Uncle Bill that she could pass on to her Trotskyite friends. But when I thought about this, it did not seem to matter. I thought — Why shouldn't she, if we are not in love, and what we are doing is for our own advantage?

Or even — If it helps to make love.

However — But if it is difficult, do I love her then?

I said 'Perhaps I do love you.'

She said 'Love me!'

Sheila had a way of looking at me when I said things like this as if she were protecting herself from torpedoes. The torpedoes were any words of tenderness that I might launch towards her.

I thought — For in love, might not the experience be overwhelming and thus castrating too?

She said 'Use your hands.'

I said 'I am.'

She said 'That's better.'

I thought — If you don't feel happy, smile: don't wait to

smile till you feel happy.

Or — Do you know the story of Miss Paragon and the Belgian Schoolgirls?

When I did in time manage to make love to Sheila she did become soft, compliant; almost like another person. I thought — One day I will know someone who from the beginning is hot and dusty and like a nut in front of a fire.

Sheila said 'Oh God that's fine!'

I thought — But in love, O God, one would not be thinking of one's own performance.

Sheila put her head back and opened her mouth like people do in films.

I think I could always make love to Sheila after a time because we distanced ourselves from ourselves and from each other: we were runners coming into the last straight: seeing her head roll, I knew I could pass her. Or we were the judges with our record-books and stop-watches: it was in the performance that there was power.

I do not know how much in this we were in fact influenced by films. In films there are bodies writhing like caterpillars because there has to be activity in front of cameras: you cannot be still: you cannot portray the nervous system. But men in films do not often seem to have erections. If one wanted to film the thing truly, one would have to go inwards; like a hand finding another hand at the beginning of a journey.

Sheila opened her eyes and looked at me fiercely; as if she were the figurehead of her ship and were turning and considering embracing it.

'Was that all right for you too?'

'Yes.'

'You promise?'

I said 'Yes!'

I thought — You should have learned not to ask that!

Then when I lay back again I wondered — Does it always have to be such a risk? Would I not rather be picked up, sometimes, and pushed as if in a pram towards the sea —

I said 'Don't go!'

She said 'I'm not going to go!'

20

She used to sit up on the bedsprings and light a cigarette.
She said 'Why don't you like me to go?'
I thought — If you picked me up and pushed me, would I
drown?
I said 'Oh, because I am the tortoise and you are the hare.'
I thought — Where did that come from: that's clever!
When Sheila got to her feet and moved about the room she
had that odd bird-like walk of women with no shoes and no
clothes on: as if their bodies have not quite got used to being
out of water.
Then she came back to the bedsprings and poked at me with
her foot. She said 'All right. Give!'
'Give what?'
'Tell me.'
I had wondered — But would I in fact like it, if she tried to
get something out of me?
She said 'You like that don't you — '
I said 'Tell you what.'
I thought — It is this that is like being put in a pram and
pushed towards the sea?
She said 'About your uncle.'
'What about my uncle?'
'Who pays his bills?'
I said 'What bills.'
She said 'He can't live as he does on his salary.'
She stood on my stomach; balancing there on one foot.
I thought — Is Eros, seen from the bottom, like a female
wrestler? Then — This is a game.
Then — Well men do like this, don't they?
I said 'I swore never to tell — '
She said 'Then never do.'
She stepped off me.
I thought — Oh dear.
I could say to Dr Anders — This is why politics is like sex
then?
Sheila said 'You wouldn't know about politics if it was under
your nose like a smell.'
I was thinking — But wouldn't it be better if politicians

21

knew they were in the business as it were for the sake of the smell?

She came and put her foot on me again.

I said 'Ow!'

Then — 'The Libyans.'

She said 'The Libyans!'

She took her foot off me.

Then she said 'What do you mean, the Libyans?'

She seemed to have been hurt.

I had meant it as a joke — That is where my uncle gets his money from.

I had been thinking — Well, I suppose it's true Uncle Bill can't live as he does on his salary.

Sheila's face seemed to have become flattened as if someone had sat on it. I was not quite sure if she was still acting, or was anxious because she was not.

I said 'Why did you ask me then?'

I thought I should explain — It just came into my head, a joke about the Libyans!

She said 'Why shouldn't I?'

She went to the window and looked out.

I was not sure what was happening.

I had thought of another thing I could say to Dr Anders — If this is the only way in which human beings can make love, is it also the only way they can alter things — by letting out the things that just come into their heads?

I said 'Have you got a pencil?'

I had at the same time thought — But isn't there another very interesting thing here, which is that if all politics is like this sort of sex divorced from love, then isn't it the case that each side wants to be the one that's lying down, while the other side is on top —

Sheila said 'What do you want a pencil for?'

I said 'I got too many things coming into my head. I've got to write them down.'

When Sheila came back and stood over me her face still seemed to have been wounded. I thought — But it was you, wasn't it, who wanted to break up the game?

22

Also — Is it only in literature then that you can say two or more things at once?

And then — There really are girls who like to kick people and people who want to be kicked —

She said 'You and the bloody things in your head!'

I got up and looked in my clothes for a pencil. Then I prowled around the room.

She said 'What is it you want to write down?'

I said 'That each side of politics is the one that wants to be lying down. But for custom's sake, each has to pretend that it's the one that wants to be on top.'

Then Sheila said 'Are you using me?'

I found a pencil. I began writing.

I said 'No.'

Then I thought — Why did she say that?

I looked up at her.

I thought — This is what happens when the game stops?

She said 'Because don't.'

I said 'And that's why people are so awful, because they're never at home in what they like.'

Sheila was standing like the prow of a ship again: a big girl, shining, with water in her eyes.

IV

The party for Mr Perhaia, the Asian or African Prime Minister, was to take place at 10 Downing Street, where Uncle Bill and Aunt Mavis and I were to be driven after we had had supper on trays at Cowley Street. Uncle Bill and Aunt Mavis and Mrs Washbourne often had supper on trays: they would try to time their meals at home in order to coincide with current-affairs programmes on television; which they took trouble to watch as if by this they might find out what was going on in the world which to some extent they were supposed to be ordering.

I had been asked to go to the reception for Mr Perhaia I think because there was little social life at Cowley Street in which I could be included, and Uncle Bill and Aunt Mavis must have felt (they were wrong) that I might mind about this. At this reception there were going to be writers and artists, Uncle Bill had said, because Mr Perhaia had himself once written a book upon cultural anthropology, and was thus supposed to like the company of intellectuals. I do not think Uncle Bill now had much time for books himself: I had once been reading in the drawing room at Cowley Street and he had come up to me and had taken the book out of my hands and had turned the back towards him to look at the title, and then had handed the book back to me as if he were just giving it clearance through the customs.

In my family I had for some reason always been supposed to be literary: I think this was because of my way of not speaking very much, and when I did, of its having been such a struggle that it had been worth my while to have tried to think of something witty.

When Uncle Bill had told me about my coming to Mr Perhaia's party — he had come across me on the landing when I had been trying to get to the bathroom as usual without being seen — he had said 'All the medusas and flatworms will be there.' This was a reference to a conversation I had with him some time before, when I had said that it seemed to me that writers and artists were like coelenterates, whose mouths are the same as their anuses. Uncle Bill had said 'I must remember that for the Royal Academy dinner.' I used to get on quite well like this with Uncle Bill. Of course I tried to charm him, as everyone did, because he was Prime Minister.

When we left the house at Cowley Street for Mr Perhaia's party there was a chauffeur and a big black car and a detective going from the back door to the front and jumping in almost as the car was moving. A few people on the pavement were waving and shouting at Uncle Bill: I think it was something to do with Mr Perhaia. Mr Perhaia was either popular or unpopular with regard to Central Africa; I was not sure which; he was temporarily a celebrity. I think politicians get pleasure from all sorts of publicity because they are people who have been brought up to need just to be the centre of attention; and detectives and big black cars and people on the pavement cheering or booing are like the toys in the nursery that their mothers either did or did not give to them.

I sat on the back seat of the car between Aunt Mavis and Uncle Bill. Mrs Washbourne, it had been made clear, was being driven separately. This was a time when efforts were being made to make Uncle Bill and Aunt Mavis seem happily married. The three of us sat straight-backed in a row; like those toys which have spikes up their arses to make them, I suppose, look pleased and upright and respectable.

In Downing Street there was another small crowd and flashing lights and a thin sort of cheering. Uncle Bill was to get out first; after Uncle Bill there would come Aunt Mavis who would have to climb out over me; and lastly myself. I had been instructed in all this: there were ways of doing things as there had been in the nursery. When Uncle Bill was on the pavement he appeared not quite to know where he was: as if he had been dumped there like a genie out of his bottle. Thus he could appear somewhat half-witted as well as magical; so people would not envy him. Then he seemed to remember to put a hand out for Aunt Mavis; to express solidarity. When it was my turn to emerge from the car the photographers were paying no attention to me: I was thankful, then sorry: after all, everyone has primitive gratifications. I had never been able to get an answer to the question of what clothes I should wear for the party, so I had on an old brown suit of my father's. I seemed to come out of it in tufts like celery. Uncle Bill and Aunt Mavis were posing on the pavement with their arms entwined like wisteria. Then we were going through that door and across the hall and down the corridor and it seemed as if it might be proper for us to act a bit dazed like Uncle Bill; banging off furniture as if we were balls on a pin-table; protecting ourselves like schizophrenics from the eyes that they insist are watching them.

Each time I went to Downing Street I meant to notice more of what it was like inside: but the place was so powerful; you wanted to keep your eyes down so the portraits on the walls would not get you. We went up the stairs. There were so many pictures of men in wigs it was like a brothel. Uncle Bill walked ahead with his feet turned out and that peculiar rolling gait that had made him so often portrayed in cartoons as a sea-captain: or perhaps more, I thought, like Sheila with no clothes on. He held his hands in his pockets with his thumbs pointing forward; his elbows ready to ward off things like knobs and springs or transvestites that he might bump into on his pin-table.

The reception was in a drawing room on the first floor where there were gilt chairs and pillars and Mrs Washbourne at the door in front of us. I thought we had left her in Cowley Street. Mrs Washbourne did in fact sometimes seem to be able to be in two places at once; as if she were a witch, or a part played by two actresses.

In the blue-and-gilt drawing room there were about a hundred people, mostly in dinner jackets and evening dress but some rather ostentatiously not: they were standing in twos and threes and looking round, it seemed, to see if they should be part of any group more important than their own; as if this was their job, to be always ready for some aggrandisement. They were talking as if to the group of people they were with but with their eyes and mouths turned towards the door; as if, like adventists, they were waiting for their messiah.

I thought — But what if God, like Godot, only ever sends a child?

I took a glass of champagne and drank it quickly and grabbed another as it went past. Then I went to a fireplace and put a foot up on the fender and stared down at glowing coals as if I were concentrating on some alchemical experiment there that might make me immune from intruders.

Proust had made use of this terrible world of grand people who come to parties to rub their legs together and keep themselves polished; who make noises like crickets not for the passing of information nor for love but for the sake of establishing status and location; their calling-songs being those to attract other important insects, their courting songs those to bemuse the opposite sex, their fighting songs those to scare off rivals. By becoming part of this scene and yet standing back from it Proust had made out of it his marvellous work of art: yet what did he feel about the whole activity, did he or did he not love it? Standing by my ring of fire in the gilded drawing room I thought — With even such a work of art, is it more than protecting yourself against something you dislike yet are attracted to?

I had once told Dr Anders a story of how I had been walking one day on Hampstead Heath and I had been talking to myself and I had said aloud — Oh I do love you! I had asked Dr Anders — Whom do you think I was talking to? and Dr Anders had said — I thought you said you were talking to yourself.

Someone took me by the elbow by the fireplace and said 'Now let's get out of that shell, shall we?'

It was Mrs Washbourne. She looked, as she often did, as if she were the Jack of Clubs. I thought — But, if she is in two places at once, might she be a man in drag?

I said 'No, really.'

She said 'The shrinking violet!'

She began pulling me across the room. I thought I might drop down on one hand and hang from her arm, as if I were a child, or her partner in a ballet.

27

She said 'We're not gorgons you know. We won't eat you!'

I wondered what Dr Anders would make of this. Gorgons are medusas, whose mouths are the same as their anuses.

We arrived at a group of men in a corner who were not wearing dinner jackets and some not even ties. I supposed that this was the artistic lot, brought in for Mr Perhaia.

'This is Bert — '

'Hullo Bert.'

For some reason I am called Bert; although I was christened Benjamin Ariel. My surname is Anderson.

' — who lives with Bill and Mavis.'

'*Who* lives with Bill and Mavis — ?'

' — Dies for England!'

They were talking to, or about, Mrs Washbourne. She had closed her eyes and was leaning back like someone trying to solve a crossword puzzle.

I was on the edge of the group, standing first on one leg and then on the other. I thought — I will slowly topple sideways; like a Tower of Pisa made out of plasticine.

'Tell us the dirt Nellie.'

'I don't know any dirt.'

' — I'm jutht theventeen — '

' — and never been — '

' — oh don't say that!'

' — kiththed — '

' — or kinned — '

' — but never less than kind — '

I had never heard people talk like this before to Mrs Washbourne. I thought I should try to like these people. They were doing some sort of cross-talk act: as if this were the best they could do in the circumstances. But there was something desperate about them: as about the comedian who puts his arm round his own neck and drags himself off the stage.

'Who's going to be Archbishop of Canterbury Nellie?'

'Are you going to be Archbishop of Canterbury Nellie?'

'Can't one be a suffragan from having been a suffragette?'

I did not think I could after all talk to these people. They were like electricity conducted on silver paper. They might

28

curl up and fuse; like the lights going on in the theatre.

Someone new had come in at the door. It was Mr Perhaia. He was a small man with dark glasses and a white cylindrical hat. He wore a grey smock down to his knees. He began to be led round the gathering by Uncle Bill; who, beside him, was like a huge white child with an Indian nanny.

I began to dream that I might make friends with Mr Perhaia. When he was introduced to me, he would hold my hand slightly longer than was usual; and I would see behind his eyes something like a bird trying to get out.

Then we might discuss cultural and anthropological questions; such as the cricket-songs that were the customs of this strange tribe.

A voice behind me said 'Like a bird on a tea-tray.'

I was not quite sure if I had heard this right. I said 'A tea-tray?'

There had been one man in the group to whom I had been introduced who had remained slightly apart from the rest: he was wearing a dinner jacket but with a dark blue shirt: he was with a black-haired woman like a film-star. This man had stayed beside me, or slightly behind me, while the others had moved to be somewhere in the line for their introduction to Mr Perhaia.

The man said 'To pick up the crumbs fallen on the top table —'

I wanted to say — But don't you think, in India, they would be handing round whisky?

I began to stammer.

The man put his hand on my arm and his head on my shoulder and laughed.

I could not remember anyone else ever laughing before when I stammered.

I said ' — Or sliding on a shaft of sunlight between pillars on his tea-tray.'

The man lifted his head and looked at me.

I think stammerers develop, as blind people do, some instinct that compensates for the faculty they are deficient in. Insofar as there is at the back of stammering — as I think there is — a feeling that conventional language is an unsuitable medium for conveying things of importance in, so there is yet the feeling that these things might be communicated by other means — perhaps by something like the letting-out, for a moment, of a caged bird behind the eyes.

The black-haired woman like a film-star moved away.

He was a tall somewhat middle-aged man with spectacles.

After a time he said 'Yes.'

Then — 'That's right.'

Then — 'I can't think of anything else to say.'

Standing like this, and looking down into the glass of champagne in my hand, and imagining that the bubbles were like birds flying out through open windows into quiet air, I had an impression that I had had once or twice before in my life; which was that I was not only looking down at myself in a maze but was looking at myself doing this: and so I could tell myself where to go; not because I saw this exactly, but because I knew I had the ability.

Then I looked towards the fireplace where I had originally taken refuge when things had seemed about to become too much for me.

There then occurred — the man with spectacles and myself remained, I think, side by side — the incident that was to be taken up in the gossip columns over the next few days and even weeks; which the reception for Mr Perhaia would for a short time become notorious for; but which few people except myself, and I suppose the man with spectacles, in fact saw, since most people were so intent on jockeying for position for their introductions to Mr Perhaia. Mrs Washbourne had gone to the fireplace and was standing there in the way that I had stood; with one foot on the fender and a hand out to the glow; as if trying to work some magic there; as if she had removed me from the fireplace almost deliberately in order to do this. And then she seemed to be tearing something up, and then to be trying to burn it, on the fire. Then a man came up and knelt in front of her and put his arms round her as if to stop her. And the two of them seemed to struggle for a moment like two children who want to get, or to keep, some secret one from the other. Then Mrs Washbourne looked round as if to see if anyone was watching. And I think they both noticed me. I had not quite seen if Mrs Washbourne had got what she wanted on to the fire. Then the man kneeling hit at the side of her dress as if it had caught alight from the fire and he was trying to put it out. But it had not caught alight; and he was just pretending it had, so that this might explain his putting his arms around her. And then Mrs Washbourne did seem to step back towards the fire as if she might thus set her dress alight; and so explain why the man was struggling with her. Then people in the room did begin to notice; to turn; and by this time it did look as if Mrs Washbourne had simply fallen into the fire, and the man was nobly trying to put her out. Then Mrs Washbourne began moving towards the door. She had a hand to her head and swayed slightly. Perhaps she thought it would appear better if she seemed somewhat drunk. And the man was standing up and brushing at his trousers. Uncle Bill was saying 'What happened?' Someone said 'Nellie fell into the fire.' Mrs Washbourne went out of the room. Uncle Bill watched where she had gone. He said 'Who pulled her out?' Then — 'Little Tommy Stout?' And everyone began laughing. And Mr Perhaia was watching with his small bird-like eyes. It was thus that the story got about that Mrs Washbourne had been drunk and had fallen into the fire, and had been saved by a secret-service man or somesuch. The man might indeed have been a secret-service man: but Mrs Washbourne had not fallen into the fire. She had been tearing something up, and the man had tried to stop her. But people were not interested in this: they were interested, as I kept telling Dr Anders, in making up stories to amuse or to protect themselves. And this was a suitable story, because a lot of people did not like Mrs Washbourne and thus were happy for her to have set fire to herself when drunk. But what I did not understand was why I used this incident myself as a chance to move away from the man who had meant so much to me; whom I liked; who had put his head on my shoulder when I had stammered; and it was only later that I worked out that perhaps I had done this because I was protecting myself; being not yet quite ready, like Icarus, to fly so close to the sun.

V

'Just laughed — '

'Yes.'

'But kindly — '

'Yes.'

'And what did you feel?'

'At first I didn't believe it. Then it was as if I were sort of above myself: seeing myself looking down on a maze.'

'A maze — '

'Yes. As if I saw myself as something in which I could find my way.'

I thought — A maze: amaze: these connections are in our minds: but are there threads in the outside world by which we find our way?

I said 'But all this stuff about spies and security men is such rubbish. It's in people's minds: they have to make up stories about these things: like once they had to make up stories about gods. There have to be free and mysterious beings who move outside fate and outside responsibility and are supposed to cause things: whom human beings would like to be like, but also wouldn't, because of the responsibility.'

Dr Anders said 'But I thought you said they didn't.'

'Didn't what?'

'Make up stories about spies and security men. They said Mrs Washbourne was drunk and fell into the fire.'

I thought — These thin green walls; the jungle; what did it look like when I looked down on the maze?

I said 'Well they'd have talked about spies and security men if they'd seen it. But they didn't. Perhaps they talk about spies and security men when in fact people are drunk, and about people being drunk when in fact they are spies and security men.'

I thought — But what I am really trying to say is that none of this matters.

Then — But why do I talk about it so much?

She said 'But it's you who are talking about spies and security men.'

I said 'I saw it.'

She said 'What did you see?'

'I've told you.'

'You've told me you saw a man kneel down by the fire and put his arms round Mrs Washbourne.'

'I suppose you think he was assaulting her.'

'It's not me who's suggested he was assaulting her.'

'You think it's me who's always thinking analysts are thinking people are doing things like assaulting people.'

Dr Anders said nothing.

What analysts do is make you feel you are tied up in knots. Or rather, they watch you while you make yourself feel tied up in knots. They encourage you almost. They do this because with other people you have found yourself tied up in knots; and you cannot begin to untie yourself, it seems, until you have some sort of model of what your knot is; and it is this that an analyst gives you, almost puts you in, so you can learn to get out.

I said 'It was in the evening paper that she was saved by some sort of secret-service or security man.'

There was Dr Anders' bookcase, her frieze, the spire beyond her window.

I thought — What I am learning is not just to think that this stuff does not matter, but to act as if it did not.

She said 'Look. There were a lot of interesting people at that party. There were interesting things going on. There was Mr Perhaia, whose influence is vital in — what — matters of life and death in Central Africa. There's your Uncle Bill, who's involved in these negotiations with the unions. And even if you weren't interested in any of this, there were what you call these artistic people: you could have got yourself introduced to any of them: you could have talked to Mr Perhaia about anthropology, whose book you say you admire.'

I said 'I know.'

33

She said 'You know what?'

I thought I might say — Nothing.

Or — Help me: there are birds that sometimes fly around the spire outside your window.

She said 'What you were interested in was being indignant about other people making up stories about spies and security men. But in fact it was you who were making up these stories, and they were making up other sorts of stories.'

I thought — All right: I have told you I know this: I will not say anything more. And I will not come back to you after the end of this session.

Dr Anders and I sometimes remained silent for several minutes.

The spire seemed to be at an angle against passing clouds; like the stick of a firework in a bottle.

I thought — But was I not going to say — Of course I'm the same as them!

— But I wasn't, was I?

— Wasn't going to say it? or wasn't the same?

Dr Anders' bookcase had all those words in them trapped between covers like birds in cages.

At my first interview with Dr Anders — after she had said the thing about what I was protecting myself from by my stammer might not be other people's disapproval but my own high opinion of myself — it had seemed clear to me that I should become her patient; and I was ready to accept this. But then towards the end of the interview, after she had taken notes about my upbringing and schooling and things like that, I had said — 'Will you take me on?' she had said — 'I myself am giving up private patients, but there are plenty of other therapists.' And I had thought — But that's wrong! and then — I'll make you! and then quickly — Of course, that's not the way. And then, rather belatedly — Of course, I can't make you. And we had gone on talking about the past, about other therapists, about the ways in which I either did, or did not, want to get rid of my stammer. And then she had raised her hands from the sides of her chair which I suppose I knew even then was her sign that the interview was nearly over. But I did not move. I was sitting opposite her. I was intent on trying to see what would happen: I felt I was almost able to watch myself in the maze. And it seemed as if she, with her hands on the arms of her chair, were on some sort of parallel bars: while I, with the part of myself that watched, was on a tightrope in my own head: with a drop on one side of — But you must take me on! and on the other of — I don't care whether you take me on or not. Either of which could be both true and untrue. Because I had to stay on the tightrope. And if I balanced well enough I could. And so we were both of us waiting. For whatever would happen. And then Dr Anders got up. She went to the door ahead of me. I followed. She put her hand on the knob of the door, as later she seemed often to be doing, and she kept her head down, and seemed to make a faint mewing sound. I thought — Don't witches work with cats? Then she said 'I might have a vacancy.' I said 'Thank you.' She said 'Monday to Friday each day three-thirty.' I said 'That's good.' She said 'Starting next week.' I said 'Fine.'

There were the clouds going past the spire beyond her window.

The window was like that painting of a painting hung in a window of a window with clouds going past it.

I said 'I know it's true I didn't want to talk to anyone at that party. I hate those parties: I always have. The people there are different from me. I don't know if I hate the people, or I hate my being different. But even when I meet someone I like I can't talk at that sort of party. People there aren't talking at all: they're just making noises to get reactions: or to stop themselves reacting. And I know I make up stories about spies and security men: but this is a sort of joke: I do it to defend myself I suppose: it's a way of trying not to take any of the things they care about too seriously. It's a way of trying to say — Look, it's all in the mind: but I know it and you don't. Oh I know I'm lonely. Other people take protecting themselves so seriously. And then they put it on to the world. So in fact there are things like spies and security men. Like vultures. Like carrion. But there wouldn't be if people said — Look, this isn't exciting, it's silly. And it's true I liked that man but couldn't think of anything to say to him. But I think there are more important things than saying: and I think he knew this too. And I think he knew I knew it. And I think there are these sort of people even if I don't speak to them much: I mean who know this sort of thing, even if they don't speak much too. Like me. And I think there's some sort of network, understanding, like this; that has some sort of life of its own; which if I chased, it might go away; but if I don't, I might find it. And it's this that matters: of which politics is only a shadow. And I can't help it if this sounds confused or silly or mysterious: it's just what I think is true.'

Dr Anders said ' — Yah boo sucks — '

I said 'What do you mean, Yah boo sucks?'

She said, as if perhaps speaking with my own voice — ' — That'll teach you to say I've been naughty! — '

I thought — Well, didn't you say I'd been naughty?

She said, as if now in someone else's voice ' — Not liking the people that mummy says you should like at parties! — '

I tried to think about this. Sometimes Dr Anders would talk as if she were playing another person's role — that of myself, or my mother, or some other powerful figure in my unconscious.

I said 'You mean, you don't think I should have liked most of those people at the party?'

She said 'Good heavens, why should you?'

I said 'I thought you said I should.'

She said 'Yes I know you did.'

I tried to go back in my mind about this. I was sure she had said — but what? — this didn't seem to matter.

I said 'But you did say, there were all those interesting people — '

'I did say, there were people who could be called interesting. I didn't say you should like them.'

I thought — This is unfair? But perhaps my mother had been unfair. So — What could I learn from this?

I said 'You mean, it's because I've been made to feel guilty about not liking these sort of people that I make up hostile stories about spies and security men?'

I thought — And I stammer?

She said 'There are after all pretty awful people at those parties.'

After a time I said 'They run the world.'

She said 'They run certain aspects of certain parts of the world.'

I thought — You mean you agree, it would be better if I stopped worrying that I don't think things that go on at those parties important?

Then — Even my mother did not really want me to feel guilty?

So — Why do I stammer?

I said 'But through these sort of people other people either die, or don't die, in Africa.'

She said 'Good heavens, don't people either die, or don't die, anyway, in Africa?'

I thought — But now, I have not stammered?

I said 'Because of this I stammered?'

— A dead body, beside some railings —

Dr Anders said 'You were a very clever little boy. It was difficult for you to take all this on when you were seven.'

I thought — Did she say very?

She said 'Wasn't your mother often worrying about who was or was not dying in Africa?'

I thought — But was she not right?

Dr Anders said 'And your father was — what — making jokes? making films?'

I thought — But was not he right too?

Then — Should I not make jokes? And should I not care?

Dr Anders said 'I just think you might try to look at these people more closely: to see them as not gods nor devils.'

I said 'Yes.' Then 'I see.'

Then — 'The people at the party?'

She said 'If you like.'

I said 'And my father and mother — '

She said nothing.

I said 'And not go on about them.'

I lay as if in my cocoon; my cot in front of the fire.

She said 'You go on with what you like.'

I thought — And are there not huge hands that hang like nests in bags from trees —

I said 'It's not that I think they're all wrong and I'm all right.

I know I sometimes sound as if I do.'

She said 'Why not.'

— A bright spring day. A pond. A poplar tree —

I said 'When I stammer, it's like some giant in my head, that I either have to kill, or be killed by.'

I thought — What was that image?

There were pigeons beyond her window, flying around the spire.

I said 'But there's one thing that really terrifies me — '

I waited for her to say something like — What?

I said 'You know, that first day, when I came to see you — '

She said 'Yes.'

I said 'And you said, about my high opinion of myself — '

She said nothing.

I said 'I had an image the other day of everyone being so much happier when they were sort of underneath, like servants or victims.'

I found myself shaking.

She said 'And you think you're not.'

I said 'I think I don't want to be.'

There were the hoofbeats up and down my spine; like the Gadarene swine rushing towards the cliff.

I said 'And when I stammer I only pretend to be.'

I thought — Not to stop myself being killed; but to stop myself killing?

I said 'To stop myself taking the responsibility.'

I thought — The responsibility — but for what?

When I looked at her she was sitting beside me with her face in profile like one of those huge statues I had seen pictures of by the banks of the Nile: staring out over the desert; or the water; or whatever it is; or nothing.

I said 'Don't you think that's terrifying?'

She had that way of pursing her lips as if making her ledge on a mountain; or preparing to play the flute.

She said 'It would certainly be unfortunate, I suppose, to have a terrifying view of servants or victims.'

VI

Sometimes after I had been to Dr Anders there was so much going on in my head that I wanted to shout and sing in the street: to say — Icarus, Icarus, you need not have flown too close to the sun! You could have pretended to be something practical like a fighter-pilot in the Battle of Britain.

When I got to Sheila's house there was a man in white overalls doing something with a screw-driver to the front door. I thought — If he is a secret-service agent or security man, will he go away if I insist that such dragons are only in my head?

Sheila's room was on the first floor. From time to time other people seemed to share it with her. I was not sure whether or not these were lovers.

I said 'I see you are being put under electronic surveillance.'

She said 'What, has the old witch finally got you?'

I said 'Don't you know about this? There aren't things like ordinary spies any more. There are just microphones and cameras and things, so that people can watch and hear everything going on everywhere.'

Sheila said 'I once knew a man like that. He was carried away in a strait-jacket.'

I went to the window and looked out. There was the top of the man's head by the front door: beyond him in the street people moved as if they were in a science fiction film and their bodies had been taken over by people from Andromeda.

I said 'So it's exactly the same as if there weren't any microphones and cameras and things, because it takes exactly the same number of people to watch and hear everything as it does to do it.'

Sheila went out of the room. After a time her head appeared below beside that of the man in white overalls. She seemed to be arguing with him. Their heads appeared enlarged; their bodies tapered like tadpoles. After a time the man swam off down the street.

I sat on Sheila's spare bedsprings and bounced up and down. I wondered — If there were a man living here who was her lover, would there, or would there not, be a mattress on the spare bedsprings?

Sheila's bed was on the opposite side of the room. I thought I could examine the pillow for hairs.

I wondered — Do people do things like this because in fact they are jealous, or because they have seen people doing things like this in films?

When Sheila came back I said 'What was all that about?'

She said 'What was all what about?'

'Do you know that man?'

'He said he'd come to the wrong house.'

Sheila sat on the bed opposite. She put her head in her hands.

After a time I said 'I've been examining your pillow.'

Sheila said 'Oh God, you're so boring, boring! Is there anything you don't make a joke of?'

I wondered — Would it help her if I exhibited jealousy by jumping up and down?

I began to take my shoes off.

I thought — But there really are men sitting underground with earphones on in London and Washington and Moscow. And since this is so, should one not provide them with some entertainment?

Then — But I am no longer supposed to be interested in things like spies and security men —

So — Do these phantoms spring from the same roots as being jealous then?

Sheila said 'Good God, there are people keeping us brainwashed! Who at this moment are in London and Washington and Moscow keeping us brainwashed! And all you can do is make jokes about it.'

I said 'What about the cigarette advertisements?'

She said 'What about the cigarette advertisements?'

I said 'Are you being brainwashed?'

She said 'Yes.' Then 'No.'

I thought — But she's not taking her clothes off.

She was sitting on the bedsprings with her hands between her thighs.

She said 'Do you know that between ten and fifteen per cent of the inhabitants of this country live below subsistence level? And that in most other parts of the world the proportions are infinitely higher?'

I wondered — Those figures are right?

I had been going to say — What the cigarette advertisements show, is that people don't mind much if they die.

I thought — Shouldn't I be just putting a hand on her breast; tugging at the belt of her trousers?

I said 'Wouldn't it be better for the people who you say are being brainwashed if they could make jokes about it? Then they might be free to do something practical rather than just talk about the people below subsistence level.'

I went and sat beside her on the bed. I tried to put a hand between her thighs.

I said 'Ah, the advantages of an unwashed brain — '

She said 'Oh shut up!'

It was as if there were something trapped in her; fighting, but not to get out.

She said 'Look, will you come and talk to Brian Alick?'

I said 'Why?'

Brian Alick was one of the leaders of the Young Trotskyites.

She said 'He's clever enough for you.'

I wondered again — I am clever?

She said 'There are millions of people degraded and oppressed. You can't say that's funny!'

I said 'I don't say it's funny.'

She said 'What do you say then?'

I said 'I say you can't change things just by putting one sort of organisation in place of another. You've got to free things in people's minds.'

She said 'You're a spoilt brat.'

I said 'Who said that?'

She said 'I did.'

I thought — That man in white overalls: he is her lover?

41

I said 'It's people like you and Brian Alick who get a kick from people being oppressed. If they weren't, you wouldn't know what to do with yourselves.'

I thought — That's unfair: or isn't it?

Then — I mustn't take my hand away!

Dr Anders would say — But you wanted to hit her?

Sheila said 'I just want to say I don't see how you can go on like this. If I were you, I'd simply be dead.'

I thought — But by keeping my hand on her, I am condescending, I am degrading her?

I said 'Jokes are serious. Wasn't it Brecht who said — '

Just then the man in the white overalls appeared at the door of the room. He stood there chewing, as if at the inside of his cheeks.

Sheila was saying 'What did Brecht say — '

I thought — Jokes break up old patterns —

The man in white overalls said in a sad voice — 'Brian says would Sunday evening about six-thirty be any good.'

Sheila shouted 'You fucking nit!'

The man said 'He says there's some kind of party.'

Sheila picked up a disc from a record-player and threw it at him.

The man raised one arm like the Statue of Liberty. The disc went past him like a flying saucer.

I thought — Sheila sent this man to a call box to ring up Brian Alick?

Sheila shouted 'Oh God Oh Jesus Christ!'

She was holding her head and was rolling about on the bedsprings.

Dr Anders might say — And you still did or didn't think he was her lover?

I could say — Or didn't mind?

I said 'Look, it doesn't matter — '

I thought — But that is condescending: shouldn't I really hit her? To save her from being the victim she both wants and doesn't want to be?

I said 'I don't mind talking to Brian Alick — '

Then — But o fool, is it not sweet reason that sends people mad?

Sheila got up and made a dash for the door. She went past the man in white overalls like King Kong. We could hear her clattering down the stairs. Then there was the noise of a door slamming — it seemed, of the bathroom.

Sheila had looked rather beautiful when she had been rolling about on the bed; like Kali, the hideous Indian goddess; who, when you rolled her over, became the beautiful goddess Devi.

The man in white overalls had gone and sat down on the spare bedsprings. He seemed to have chewed enough on his cheeks and was doing some swallowing.

I said 'What were you doing to the front door?'

He said 'Putting in an entryphone.'

I said 'Good God, what would anyone in this house want with an entryphone?'

He said 'You can speak into it downstairs and then people upstairs know who you are.'

I thought — This man, like any comedian, is either half-witted or witty.

He was like some famous actor, I couldn't remember the name. This actor had a long face and pale curly hair and he specialised in roles of terrible despair and bitterness. Once a group of his friends had taken the front row of the stalls, and had worn mackintoshes.

I said 'Why would Sheila want to know who's coming up the stairs?'

The man said 'I think she's a bit fed up you don't come and live with her.'

I thought — That's true? Then — That's all right then?

I said 'She's never said that.'

He said 'Well, she wouldn't, would she.'

I thought — O God, do I mean it is all right because I am the one on top and we neither of us are happy —

There was a noise of things being smashed up in the bathroom.

I said 'You really think that?'

He said 'It sounds like it doesn't it?'

I thought — Then can I go and say — But Sheila, Sheila, you only think you want me to come and live with you because you

43

think I'm happy!

The man said 'She tried to take an overdose the other day.'

I said 'Damn!'

I got up and went out of the room and down the stairs to a landing. I stood outside the bathroom door.

I thought — But how can I say just — Sheila, Sheila, I don't care about any of this! I don't care about the man in white overalls! I don't care if you've been lying —

I pushed on the door. It was locked. I said 'Sheila — '

I thought — But if I say Sheila, Sheila, I do care about all this: if I was lying, would it help? Would I not have to break the door down to prove it?

Also — Even if I do break the door down, won't she feel guilty because she's made us so fantastical?

I said 'Sheila, I would like to talk to Brian Alick.'

I thought — I have locked myself behind bathroom doors like this often enough in my life, God knows: I should know what to do about it.

I said 'I want to talk about Marxism.'

I remembered — You have to get what is trapped in the mind out onto something different.

I said 'I want to ask him whether or not Marx in fact said that the victory of the working class was inevitable.'

After a time Sheila said 'Of course he didn't say it was inevitable!'

I said 'What did he say then?'

There was the sound, through the bathroom door, of the seat of a lavatory being raised or lowered.

I thought — This is the point of politics then? To comfort people in, or get them out of, lavatories?

Sheila said 'He said it might be historically inevitable, but that didn't mean you didn't have to work for it.'

There was the sound of a lavatory flushing.

Sheila said 'And anyway, what he said was in an historical context.'

I could say to Dr Anders — Politics, you see, is what people talk about when they are afraid that there is no meaning; that the birds behind their eyes might have died —

Sheila said 'Will you go away now please.'

I said 'Yes.'

She said 'And you'll come and see Brian on Sunday.'

I said 'Fine.'

I thought — When I am gone, she will be able to come out and pretend at least to herself that she has been peeing.

She said 'About five-thirty. Here. First.'

There was the sound of a bath beginning to run.

I said 'See you.'

I went down the stairs. I made a noise like a body clattering.

I thought — But where are feelings then?

I wondered — Do birds have their own feelings, like exercises, to keep alive; when they are on their own, behind closed doors, behind the eyes?

VII

Often at weekends Uncle Bill and Aunt Mavis would be away and I would be on my own in Cowley Street except for the housekeeper who came in for a while each day and one or two secretaries who went in and out of the basement and with whom I need have no contact if I was careful.

I would look forward to being on my own: then sometimes I could not think of any reason to get out of bed, and would lie like the donkey between the two bundles of hay that seemed to exist only in my imagination.

I did not want to ring Sheila now: not especially, I think, because I minded about the man in white overalls, but perhaps because I minded about not minding.

Depression, I think, is not so much a feeling, as a sort of impression it would be better to have no feelings at all.

I can hardly remember this now, with all the profusion!

The work that I was supposed to be doing in preparation for a university was philosophy. I tried to read my books in bed. I held them on my stomach as if they were shields that might protect one part of my body from another.

The philosophy I was reading was that of the Sceptics: who held that one explanation of something was likely to be no more valid than another: whose favourite words were 'perhaps' and 'possibly' and 'maybe': who thought that it was necessary to 'suspend judgement' for the sake of mental health. They considered anyone who thought himself capable of conclusive judgement to be mentally unbalanced. I found this philosophy encouraging: but did not quite feel, at the moment, that I had found the right way of demonstrating mental health.

I would think — How exciting it should be that there are no better reasons for the sun to rise rather than not rise every morning! That as I lie in bed, I equally may or may not fall through to the floor!

— Especially when the sun always does rise every morning: and I never do fall through to the floor.

What philosophers who were not sceptics were saying, it seemed to me, was that although they agreed that reason could not make final judgements, yet nevertheless we had to live as if it could; so our lives were ridiculous anyway.

So the only question that remained was whether or not we faced this.

One could spend so much time ruminating upon these things that although one might be incapable of getting out of bed, at least one was not worried by all the things that Uncle Bill and Mrs Washbourne were worried about — such as whether or not oil was getting through to Africa, or who was getting what percentage of which money.

I would wonder about all this with the books that I held balanced on my stomach seeming increasingly to cut off the top part of my body from the lower.

I knew — Then my lower part, yes, begins to lead a life of its own; to wake up and moan like a baby; finally to scream and yell as if it has been left too long without food.

Then I would think — But how can I feed it? What is this need, when I am on my own, that stops me reading interesting things like philosophy?

I had a small store of pornographic literature in my room which I kept in a box in a cupboard. It lay there like some great spider; which every now and then came out to feed when either I, or it, was hungry.

I had had a conversation with Dr Anders about this. She had said 'Why are you ashamed of pornography?' I had said 'Because it makes me feel ill.' She had said 'Why do you read it then?' I had said 'Because at least I know where I am, when I feel ill.'

I had wanted to ask — Don't other people find that?

— Because like this their tensions have run out? they are in their mother's arms again?

As I lay in bed I would make efforts to join up the one half of my body with the other. There was a feeling like a rugger scrum composed of my head and my groin. This particular Sunday —

47

the one after the Friday I had talked to the man in white overalls with Sheila — I thought I should try to jump out of bed and do something practical like go down to Uncle Bill's study and see whether or not there was a hole in the ceiling caused by his pistol going off. But according to the Sceptics, how would I know, even if there was a hole, that it had been caused by a pistol? And according to psychoanalysis, how would I know that I was not in fact thinking about masturbation?

Dr Anders had said — It's masturbation that makes you feel ill? I had wanted to say — Oh I know that's no reason to think there's anything wrong in it!

I tried to jump out of bed. The messages could not quite get through to my muscles from my brain.

I thought — There are men with guns lined up on the ground to shoot down these carrier pigeons.

One of the books of philosophy that I admired that was not to do with the Sceptics, was Plato's *Phaedrus*. Here images lived a life of their own: they seemed to be free even within the cages of reasoning. There was the image of a person being someone in a chariot pulled by two horses, the one good and the other bad. It was the bad horse that pulled a person down from the road to the gods along which the good horse was taking him: but it was also this dark horse that enabled him perhaps to get back on to the road to the gods again: for it would be the dark horse that dragged him to recognise, and thus to make contact with, his beloved: and so he grew wings, and was reminded of the gods again.

Dr Anders would say — Did Plato really say that?

I would say — Well, it seems to me he did.

I wondered if it would help me to get out of bed and go down to Uncle Bill's study if I pretended to myself that what I was going to do was to get at my small store of pornography; then when I was on my feet I could make a dash for the study; so that it would have been my dark horse that had got me back on the road to the gods again.

I had such a terrible ache in my head, my groin: I thought — This is a suspension of judgement?

— Oh where was my beloved!

I thought — What terrible battles are fought like Hastings or Waterloo halfway across the floors of bed-sitting-rooms towards cupboards!

I was like a man being beaten up by police on television. I could say — All right! I give in! What I wanted was just the story of Miss Paragon and the Belgian Schoolgirls —

Was this in fact why people were beaten up by police? because they, or the police, were, or were not, ashamed of their stores of pornographic feelings?

Oh come on, come on, my dark horse; take me to my beloved!

I was making such an effort to get my dressing-gown on and to reach the door of my bedroom that I thought my mind might tear with the weight round the nails through it.

I thought — Oh where is the bird that must have perched on that loved one's shoulder then!

There was a sort of scraping noise coming from behind the walls in the direction of the attic.

I thought — That old spider, in my head, my groin, is scratching in the attic?

I had moved on to the landing, with caution, to see who might be there.

I thought — A plumber?

But then — Does not this word now refer to someone fixing up electronic surveillance?

I could say to Dr Anders — Just tell me, will you, how I get away from all these images?

— The birds falling down from the sky like shot pigeons —

Would in fact it be better, if one just masturbated in the attic?

There should not be anyone in this part of the house at weekends. I wondered — Might the shot from Uncle Bill's study have gone right through Aunt Mavis's bedroom and up into the roof? and there is a man mending the hole there?

As I was watching the door into the attic the handle began to turn.

I thought — In films, this shot would be too corny; but it is still alarming.

The door opened. A man with crinkly hair looked out. When he saw me he seemed upset.

He said 'They didn't tell me!'

I began stammering.

I thought — He'll think I'm gibbering with fear.

He went to the staircase and looked down. He was wearing a tweed jacket and grey flannel trousers.

He said 'Are there any more of you?'

I wanted to say — Of course not!

He said 'I was supposed to have done this job last week. I'll get into trouble if they know I'm doing it now.'

He looked at me accusingly. He was a sad, quiet man. I thought — I should try to reassure him?

I wanted to say — Well I won't tell anyone.

I thought I could explain — It'll be all right for both of us, won't it, if it's the fact after all that you're fixing up the hole in Uncle Bill's ceiling —

I said 'The hole — '

He said 'The hole.'

Then — 'Yes.'

When he looked at me he had absolutely nothing behind his eyes; or behind his words, or his inflexions.

I thought — If he were in a film, wouldn't he be wondering whether or not to kill me?

Then — Of course I am not really frightened.

He said 'You're here at weekends?'

I said 'Yes.'

He said 'What do you do?'

I said 'Philosophy.'

He frowned.

I thought — Well, according to the Sceptics, is not one answer as good as another?

Then — But am I not the person who knows something is going on behind the stage; and so in a different dimension.

He said 'Look, if they knew I was here, I'd lose my job.'

I still wanted to say — Well I won't tell anyone.

Dr Anders would say — Well why didn't you?

I said — 'You mean you don't want me to tell anyone?'

He said 'Right.'

Dr Anders might say — You really did think he might do

something to you?

I thought — Am I not trying to help him?

The man said 'Those cows! They call it information!'

Then he went back into the attic.

There still had been no intelligible messages coming from behind his eyes.

I went down the stairs. I was still carrying my clothes. I had no shoes. I thought I might go into Uncle Bill's bedroom and borrow his slippers.

I could have said to the man — Let's say you're a plumber; if a plumber had not been a man fixing up electronic surveillance.

I was putting on my clothes on the landing outside Uncle Bill's bedroom. I thought I might take the opportunity to go and look at his floors and ceilings.

I could say to Dr Anders — But what else could the man have been doing? Other than mending a hole in the ceiling?

And if this were true, it was true they would not want it known —

— Or could he be my white horse to divert me from my beloved!

I was going on down the staircase.

On the pavement, outside the front door, there was one of the policemen put on to guard Uncle Bill. I could go up to him and say — There is a man who might be a plumber or a masturbator in the attic —

But Uncle Bill would not want even a policeman to know, if there was someone mending a hole in his ceiling.

I thought — Perhaps we inoculate ourselves with these hideous images to save ourselves from more simple pornography.

I was shuffling along the pavement towards Victoria Street. I could not quite remember how I had got there. I was wearing Uncle Bill's bedroom slippers. I had looked into Uncle Bill's bedroom and study briefly, but there had not seemed to be any holes in floors or ceilings. I had not spoken to the policeman at the front door, who had smiled at me.

I could explain to Dr Anders — But still, there is some sense in all this: I am out in the air: perhaps it is true that the mental health of the Sceptics is in not expecting to be able to judge between this and that explanation —

I was moving parallel to Victoria Street, between it and the river. It was a bright windy day. People in the street were going past like leaves blown from Andromeda.

There were some pornographic bookshops at the back of Victoria Station.

I thought — For God's sake, if I could hold out a crucifix at you, fart at you, would you stop following me?

Dr Anders would say — I thought you were on your way to your beloved —

— That dark horse, to drag me down, like a child at the skirts of its mother.

The man with crinkly hair had been so terrible! He had had such a life: his mother, like a seagull, had gone for his eyes and got him —

I thought — Should I not just have put out a hand to him and said — Get it out, get it out, it won't hurt you —

Or — Is it not the best in the best of all possible worlds, that there are these dark horses to take me to my beloved?

I had come to one of the pornographic bookshops at the back of Victoria Station. I thought — You go out through a door, along a passage, and in through the same door —

The covers of the magazines seemed to have been carrying on for some time a contest about how far they could see up women's arses.

I thought — And all these men, like ghosts, in their chain-mail, clanking; who want to post things like letters up women's arses —

A voice behind me said 'Hullo.'

I said 'Oh hullo.'

'Have you got the time on you?'

He was a flat-faced man, rather elderly.

I thought I might explain — I'm here just to study the anthropology of this strange tribe; the question of why it is customary to make letter-boxes of arses —

I said 'No.'

He said 'Would you like a cup of coffee?'

I thought — Well, I would, wouldn't I?

Then — This is not a dark horse to take me to my beloved!

He said 'I know quite a good place round here.'

I thought I could explain — But I'm carrying out an experiment, you see, to discover what happens if you simply act what seems truthful —

I said 'All right.'

In fact I would like a cup of coffee.

We walked round the corner.

I thought — An experiment is not an experiment, is it, if you think you know the result —

Round the corner there was a cafe with red-topped tables and bottles of sauce like fly-traps.

He said 'You've done this before?'

I said 'No.'

He said 'You'd like some coffee?'

I said 'Yes.'

I sat at the table while he went to the counter.

I thought — There is that story about the prison warder who goes to bed with the man in the condemned cell out of pity —

Then — But I'm not his warder?

The man came back with some coffee. He said 'Here.'

I said 'Thanks.'

He said 'Where do you come from?'

I said 'Cowley Street.'

'Cowley Street!'

'Yes.'

I could say to Dr Anders — You see, I told you —

He said 'What do you do?'

I said 'Philosophy.'

We drank our coffee.

He said 'I've got a room round here.'

I thought — Dear God, perhaps I do not after all know about dark horses!

He said 'I'll give you twenty pounds.'

I said 'Twenty pounds!'

I thought — Can it possibly be true, that I would not like twenty pounds?

He was a man with such a sad flat face; as if his mother had sat on him.

I thought — But even if everything is for the best in the best of all possible worlds —

Then he said 'Haven't I seen you somewhere before?'

I said 'I don't know, have you?'

He said 'Excuse me.'

He got up and went to talk to the man behind the counter.

He seemed to pay for the coffee. Then he went out through a door at the back.

I thought — Perhaps it was the photograph of me getting out of the car at Mr Perhaia's party?

Or — Could he be all the time one of Uncle Bill's detectives put on to follow me —

I could explain to Dr Anders — But this is still the point: if you just let things happen truly, at least you get a cup of coffee.

— But perhaps I should not think that I could talk about this too much anyway.

The man behind the counter was eyeing me suspiciously.

After a time I went out into the street. There was no sign of the flat-faced man.

I thought — And I did know, all the time, that nothing unpleasant would happen, didn't I!

Then — One day there will be horses, or birds, to carry me to my beloved.

VIII

'Brian, this is Bert.'

'Hullo Bert.'

'This is Brian.'

The meeting that Sheila had arranged for me to talk with Brian Alick turned out to be taking place at a party at the house of Sally Rogers, a television personality. Sally Rogers had once been an interviewer on television; then she had become involved with the Young Trotskyites. She was now much in demand on talk-shows to give the revolutionary point of view; which she did in a way that did not upset people, talking pleasantly about the need to break up society for the good of the people in it; thus encouraging the people watching her I suppose to imagine, because she was pretty, that the sooner society was broken up the better; because there might then be a better chance for people like them to go to bed with people like Sally Rogers.

'What was it you wanted to talk to me about, Bert?'

When we had arrived at the party Sheila had taken me straight to Brian Alick: she had not even introduced me to Sally Rogers. Brian Alick was a short, compact man with smooth hair and a grey flannel suit and eyes that looked over my shoulder as if towards an autocue.

'Shall we sit here?'

When people wait for me to talk in public, it is once more as if all the lights have come on too brightly in a theatre and there is nothing for anyone to do except leave the building.

I sat with a glass in my hand and I wondered about language being useless because it could only say one thing at a time: while what things are truly is always a network of connections.

There were about twenty people in the room. It was a sort of drinks party. I was being treated as if I were on television.

I said 'Why do you think if you got power — '

There was this line of guns shooting down messages between my brain and my muscles: I thought — Is it my body that cannot bear this simplicity —

' — you would be any different from — '

— but with people who talk fluently is there not always something projected blindly like an autocue, and not a bird, behind one's head —

' — from any other communist government in power — '

My stammer was having the effect of people paying attention to me: or rather not quite to me, but slightly to one side of me, as if there might be knobs there which might adjust my programme.

'You mean — '

' — which — '

'Sorry.' This was Brian Alick.

' — can only maintain itself in power — '

Sally Rogers was watching me intently. She was a brown-faced, dry-skinned woman like a Californian tennis player.

' — by means of a secret police — '

Dr Anders had once said — You know how attractive it is when you stammer?

' — the chief aim of which is — '

I thought — This cannot be attractive!

Then — If I get out of this alive, might I get off with Sally Rogers?

' — to oppress the workers that they say they want to liberate.'

I had finished. I seemed to have taken about ten minutes. I tried not to let my breath out too heavily.

I thought — It is an effort like making love to Sheila?

Also — Did not Plato say, somewhere, that there is a vulgarity in people who are too fluent and precise?

Brian Alick waited for a time as if to make sure I had finished: then he spoke with his eyes still over my shoulder.

'I suppose we are talking about the Soviet Union. Now as you know we are opposed to the Soviet Union. We consider in fact that the Soviet Union has quite deliberately betrayed socialism — '

I thought — But with people who speak fluently, isn't it then the case that their mouths are different from their anuses?

— But still, it is the case that their mouths are where things go in —

' — as Trotsky himself said as early as 1927. No, the role of the party in a workers' socialist state — '

Sally Rogers was standing with her legs apart and was watching me as if I were one of her tennis balls in California.

' — but I need not go on about this. Take the example for instance of Chile — '

— Her legs bent slightly inwards at the knees: turn her over, and her sand would run down the other way as in an hourglass —

' — No, what we say is, give power to the British worker — the British worker who is a responsible and sophisticated political being — and you will find, once he has been liberated from the conditioning of his oppressed and oppressive past — '

'But — '

' — that he will be able to look after his own interests: and how will it be in his interests to let himself be oppressed by what will be after all his own police?'

I thought — Sally Rogers might be like Miss Paragon the Belgian Schoolmistress.

'Yes?' This was Brian Alick.

I thought — One day, you old man at my windpipe, I will get you before you get me.

'How — '

I thought — I will now do my breathing exercises: in, one two: hold it, three four: out, five six seven eight — like one of those statues that stare out, or wait to give birth, over the banks of the Nile.

'Take your time Bert.'

'How will you free him?'

'Free him?'

'The British worker. From his conditioning.'

'It will take some re-education certainly — '

'But that's — '

' — what we're planning — '

' — what would be done by — '

' — as I was saying — '

57

' — the secret police.'

I thought suddenly — Is it the point of my stammering that I won't accept that I may have to attack people?

— But still, who would be hurt?

Brian Alick said 'No. We see this as much more of a natural process when once the substructure and superstructure of an oppressive society have been taken away — '

But how —

And so on: round and round: like mice on a treadmill.

I thought — I am frightened of myself being hurt? Of Brian Alick being hurt? Of my opponent, whoever he is, lunging forwards and flying out of the window?

' — a natural process as much as a part of the processes of history — '

I thought — It is life that does the hurting; and the re-education, certainly; I should not fear it.

Then there came in at the door, as late arrivals at the party, a group of people who were like dancers coming on half way through an opera: people different from the others on the stage: very conscious of themselves, of their bodies, of how they looked and moved; in contrast to the lumpishness of an opera chorus —

' — which after all was seen clearly enough by Trotsky — '

One of the people who had come in was a girl of about my own age who wore a cap and a sort of jacket with bells —

Brian Alick's voice faded as if sound had been switched off.

— a girl with such softness, tightness about her; such a taste of dust; that at a touch she might crumble; as if exposed in a tomb after thousands of years —

The camera, my eyes, remained on Brian Alick; his lips moving like mice on a treadmill —

— someone round and compact as a nut or an internal organ —

I thought — This, then, is my dark horse? Do I feel life emerging?

— like a butterfly; a girl with such soft skin over sharp bones; a small, self-reflecting, wiry-haired girl —

Brian Alick said 'But you were saying?'

— That my heart turned over.

58

She had come in with two or three men who were older than she. They were shaggy men, like trappers, out all winter.

They went over to a table and began to eat and drink as if they were starving.

I said 'Power is to do with armies and police. That is, once you've thrown over custom and tradition. All this stuff you talk of, workers' committees and co-operation and so on, this is the talk of people with no real interest in power, who like to stay in opposition.'

Brian Alick said 'I can tell you we certainly don't intend to stay in opposition!'

I thought — Does she provide honey for those bears and bees?

I said 'Then you'll have the problem of what to do with the people who don't do what you tell them, won't you.'

I thought — Now, when I have someone to talk for —

Someone said 'But Bert, not everyone is like your uncle!'

This was Sheila.

I thought — Now, I do not stammer?

Sheila was sitting beside, and slightly behind, Brian Alick, on a sofa. She had her hand on his shoulder.

I thought — I believe that by talking like this I can attract the girl at the table?

I said 'What's wrong with my uncle? He knows about power. He doesn't shelter behind the fact that it's easier for anyone to be a sort of martyr in opposition.'

The girl at the table still had her back to me. She seemed to move slightly while remaining quite still; like a table-tennis ball on a jet of water.

Sheila said 'He shelters behind the army and the police!'

I said 'My Uncle Bill?'

I remembered Dr Anders so often saying — If you do object to people, why don't you get angry?

People were now listening to me openly. There was what seemed to be some slight confrontation.

Everyone was paying attention, that is, except the group by the table.

Sheila said 'Well take the Matanga tribe for instance — '

I thought — I will not be taking this out on Sheila just

59

because it is easy —

I said 'Oh I do think it's pathetic, to say my uncle is responsible for the Matanga! What was he at the time, one man sitting in England with bits of paper, pushing bits of paper around, what do you think he had to do with all those deaths in Africa? Do you think people wouldn't have died if there hadn't been people like my uncle pushing bits of paper around? Oh I know it was to do with guns, but do you think people won't kill each other if they want to, just if there aren't people like my Uncle Bill trying to deal with things like guns? What do you think people like my Uncle Bill do? They're helpless; they're dummies; put up by two sides of a football crowd, you know, in those scarves and funny hats, with rattles. Do you think they can make, or stop, people being killed and killing? They're not powerful. You're the people who think people like Uncle Bill are powerful, because you think you'd like to have that sort of power yourselves; but you wouldn't, you just like talk, you like people like my Uncle Bill being there for you to grumble at. What on earth would you do if you had power? If you couldn't grumble? You think there'd be fewer deaths in Africa? You don't want power; you want things neat and tidy. That only happens in talk. People like my Uncle Bill know their limitations: they say they're public servants; but don't be taken in; they really are. They watch the little bits of paper being pushed around: they chase after them. Someone has to do something with all those terrible bits of paper. But if you think people like Uncle Bill are in control, you're crazy. You're the ones who think people are in control. You don't know your limitations. You're élitist.'

I thought — Dear God, I have spoken: who cares about whether or not I am in control?

Then — Will she even now not turn to me?

— Me on my fine chariot, with my plunging horses!

After a time someone said 'Your Uncle Bill is a servant?'

I said 'Trotsky said he himself was the servant of history.'

I thought — Well he did, didn't he?

Sally Rogers had come over to me. She said in a husky voice 'Can I fill you up?'

I thought — Oh well, I will be better off with her than with Sheila, won't I; her legs like an hour-glass with the sand running down —

Brian Alick had turned away and was whispering to Sheila. Others were recomposing themselves as if after some slight accident.

Sally Rogers said 'I liked what you said.'

I said 'Did you?'

I thought — One goes where the wind takes one.

The girl by the table had still not turned to me.

I thought — I must remember, what I may well forget, that that girl will always hurt me.

Then — But what is not good, if it is where my dark horse takes me!

Sally Rogers said 'Especially the bit about servants. I mean, about people liking power in order not to be free.'

I thought — Oh well, Sally Rogers will be my good white horse then.

She said 'Come and let me get you something to eat.'

I followed her to the table. I thought — Now, if I really want to, is the time to talk to the girl with curly hair.

I said to Sally Rogers 'Ah, but without such martyrs, how would we live — '

The girl and her entourage seemed to be already moving towards the door.

I thought — Go and put your hand on her shoulder —

I said to Sally Rogers ' — Who make the water hot; the trains run on time — '

I thought — But is not the point of the experiment still to find out what is true?

I said 'What else would we talk about, in the long winter evenings?'

Sally Rogers said 'Shall I show you?'

I said 'Yes.'

The girl had gone out of the door.

IX

When I got back to Cowley Street it was Sunday evening so I expected still to be on my own in the house, but Uncle Bill and Aunt Mavis and Mrs Washbourne seemed to have returned early and there were people moving in and out of the front door like undertakers. I thought — Would it not be better if Government officials wore caps and bells like clowns? Could they not then be taken more seriously?

I thought I might go round to the back of the house and try to climb over the garden wall and in through the kitchen window: but it seemed better to save this up for when my situation might be more desperate.

'Oh Bert — '

'Yes.'

'Can your uncle have a word with you please?'

This was Mrs Washbourne. I had got past the policeman at the door: had smiled at one or two servants or dignitaries in the hall: then Mrs Washbourne had been outside Uncle Bill's study like a head prefect.

I thought — Why is one always caught like this just when one has been trying to defend the headmaster?

'Come along in. Sit down. Are you all right in your room?'

This was still Mrs Washbourne. Uncle Bill was in a corner watching television. On the screen there was a commentator talking but the sound was switched off. The commentator's lips were like mice on a treadmill.

'Did you have a good weekend?'

'Yes thanks.'

'It must be pretty lonely.'

'No I'm fine.'

I wondered if they might have found my small store of pornography.

— Or the man in the attic might have told them — but what?

'What happened to that friend you had at school?'

'Oh, he's in Greece.'

I thought — I understood whom she was talking about rather too quickly?

Then — Perhaps it's the man who tried to pick me up at Victoria Station?

I could explain — But I was carrying out this experiment, you see, to test the theory that if homosexuals act truly they do not go to bed with each other —

— But my friend and I at school had, hadn't we?

Mrs Washbourne said 'Perhaps you could have some people round here to keep you company.'

I said 'That would be nice.'

She said 'Who would you like?'

I thought — Sheila and Brian Alick?

— Or, one day, the girl with curly hair.

Mrs Washbourne was not really talking to me. She was filling in time for Uncle Bill who was watching television.

I thought — He is waiting to see if he himself comes on.

Mrs Washbourne said 'Your Uncle doesn't get much time.'

I said 'Oh that's all right.'

I thought — What happens when you two go to bed?

I do not know if I have made it clear that I liked Uncle Bill. Out of all the people I knew in the grown-up world he seemed to me to be one of the best; perhaps because he was so successful; which gave him a confidence perhaps to stand back and see himself; to see the world that he was involved in as a bit mad too; looking down on himself as if he were in the maze and there were something of that thread or the bird behind his eyes —

When Uncle Bill did switch off the television and come over to me by the fire there were such bags of exhaustion under his eyes that it was as if he might have to pick them up and carry them like suitcases.

Mrs Washbourne went to a table by the window and stood there by a machine which seemed to be a mixture between a large typewriter and the sort of computer which tells you whether or not you have a seat on an aeroplane.

Uncle Bill and I sat each side of an unlit fire.

He said 'Bert, did you have a good weekend? I'm afraid it's a bit lonely here. Are you comfortable in your room? What happened to that friend you had at school?'

I said 'He's in Greece.'

I thought — Well, it must be nice for them I suppose if they think they can show they are decent about homosexuals.

Uncle Bill said 'We must get some people round here some time. Make things more jolly for you.'

He was loosening his clothes and pulling out a pipe like a woman getting a breast out to feed a baby.

He said 'You've got these friends. What are they? Trotsky-ites. Revolutionary Socialists. Or whatever. So they tell me.'

I thought — Ah, so it's not the man at Victoria Station.

Uncle Bill stuffed his finger into his pipe. I wondered — What would Dr. Anders think I am thinking — that Uncle Bill is playing with his pipe like a child?

He said 'You're interested in their politics?'

I said 'Not really.'

He said 'No reason why you shouldn't be. When I was your age I was quite a dab hand at Marx.'

He turned and smiled at Mrs Washbourne who was in front of the machine on the table.

He said 'Have you got that thing turned off Nellie?'

Mrs Washbourne smiled; as if, like the Mona Lisa, she had sat on a sharp rock.

I thought — It's true they might be bugging themselves?

Also — That man in the attic did look like President Nixon?

Uncle Bill said 'I've never understood why, if the victory of the working class is so inevitable — '

I said 'Oh they say it isn't — '

'They do?'

'Yes. Or rather, they say it isn't when it suits them and they say it is when it suits them. They're very sensible really. You can make out Marx to say almost anything, like the Bible.'

Uncle Bill banged his pipe against the fender. I wondered — Is he impressed by this?

64

From his huge hands, bits of ash fell out on to the world.

I could not make out what Mrs Washbourne was doing. She was standing over her machine as if it were a pin-table and she was waiting to tilt it with her stomach.

Uncle Bill said 'You know your Marx?'

I said 'Not much.'

He said 'It's the moral indignation I found valuable.'

I could not quite make out what was behind Uncle Bill's eyes. It was as if they were barricaded by milk bottles piling up outside a front door.

He said 'Do they ask you personal questions?'

I said 'Personal questions?'

Mrs Washbourne had sat down by her machine. I thought — She is in fact taking this down? To be used as evidence?

Then — I am mad?

I said 'I've got this girlfriend.'

He said 'Sheila.'

I said 'Yes.'

He said 'You see, we're quite efficient.'

I thought — I am not mad?

Uncle Bill said 'Always someone behind the curtain! Always someone behind the arras!'

He smiled; and moved his pipe across his mouth as if from one breast to the other.

I thought — The man in white overalls? The man in the attic?

Mrs Washbourne was in front of her machine as if she might be waiting for some message from Andromeda.

Uncle Bill said 'As a matter of fact I get most of it from Mavis.'

I tried to work this out. He was telling me I was being watched: or how did he know of my relationship with Sheila and the Trotskyites? But he was also telling me he knew all this was a bit of a joke: since he got most of his information from Aunt Mavis.

— But anyway, what was behind the arras?

— Was Polonius a piece of electronic equipment then?

He said 'And she gets it from these gossip-column fellows.'

I said 'Oh.' Then 'Ah.'

Then — 'Has there been anything in the papers?'

He said 'Not yet.'

I thought — But he would not want me to know if I were being bugged? He would say — It's those gossip-column fellows?

— But he would say this if it was.

Uncle Bill said 'They ask you questions about what goes on in this house?'

I thought — This is all too simple.

I said 'They spend most of the time talking about who killed Trotsky.'

He said 'Who killed Trotsky?'

I said 'It seems certain that it was someone in the Russian Secret Service. But the point is that Trotskyites like to think that either one set of people or another were traitors in his entourage. This obsesses them. Keeps them occupied. Things like spies: secret-service men. You know.'

I thought — I know I'm doing this to be difficult.

— But what has happened to that bird that was once behind Uncle Bill's eyes; has it become trapped, and is dying there?

He said again 'They don't ask personal questions?'

I said 'No.'

He sucked at his pipe.

After a time I said 'I don't think they're much of a threat to you really. I mean they feel things very simply. They feel society's rotten, which it is, but they haven't any plans to make it better. They keep themselves ready for what will turn up, which is quite sensible really. That's how revolutions do happen. They do I suppose put people into trade unions and things; but these are the sort of people who would be in trade unions anyway. I mean, what's the point of a trade union if there aren't people in it who want to kick up all sorts of fuss —

Uncle Bill was looking at Mrs Washbourne. Mrs Washbourne seemed to be still poised over the keys of her machine; as if the announcement she was expecting was being shot down by angels.

I thought — The message from Andromeda might be devilish then?

Uncle Bill said 'This Dr Anders, he doesn't ask you questions?'

I thought — Good heavens!

Mrs Washbourne said 'Dr Anders is a woman.'

Uncle Bill said 'Dr Anders is a woman?'

I thought — They are mad then.

But — How wonderful it will be to tell Dr Anders that Uncle Bill thought she was a Trotskyite, and a man!

Uncle Bill was watching Mrs Washbourne. She was watching her machine. I thought — The bird that was trapped behind Uncle Bill's eyes has been dead some time?

Uncle Bill said 'Let's go back, shall we, to what we were saying before we were interrupted.'

I thought — Take that, Mrs Washbourne, behind the arras!

He said 'There are things, after all, they would dearly like to know about this house. Does he, or does she, or whoever this Dr Anders is, ask you personal questions?'

I said 'She's an analyst. Of course she asks personal questions.'

I thought — Don't you even know that?

Uncle Bill bared his teeth against his pipe as if he were trying to hurt someone.

I said 'But analysts don't really ask questions about what goes on outside. They're not really interested. They ask questions about what goes on in your mind. And then, perhaps, they try to make connections with what's outside.'

He said 'Then she does ask questions about what goes on in the house.'

I thought — What's coming from Andromeda is the madness of simplicity.

I said 'Dr Anders isn't a Trotskyite.'

He said 'Do you know that?'

I said 'Yes.'

I thought — Well, do I?

Then — Isn't this just the sort of question that Dr Anders herself would have asked?

I said again 'Yes.' Then —

— But it was too difficult, after all, to try to explain to Uncle Bill why I knew Dr Anders wasn't a Trotskyite.

He said 'It's always been my conviction that things of a

personal nature should be kept away from public life.'

I thought I might say — But you see, Dr Anders would be interested in just this —

— How can a person keep things of a personal nature away from public life?

— By tearing himself in two?

Uncle Bill said 'They don't ask you questions about what goes on in this house?'

I thought — He is tired.

I said 'There was a man doing some sort of job in the attic yesterday. Did you know?'

Uncle Bill looked at Mrs Washbourne.

Then he began banging his pipe against his knuckles so that burning ash fell over his clothes like meteorites.

I thought — He wants to immolate himself?

I said 'He didn't say what he was doing: he seemed to want not to be found out.'

Mrs Washbourne called 'Don't do that!' She left her machine and came over to Uncle Bill. She beat at his trousers as if he were on fire.

I thought — They pretend there is a fire when there is not; when they want to cover something up —

— But what will they do if there is a fire?

Uncle Bill said 'Don't do that Nellie!'

I said 'I thought I'd better tell you.'

I could say to Dr Anders — You see, I told you, they do not want to know; all this is too daft to keep one's mind on —

Uncle Bill said 'There are some bad hats I suppose in any profession.'

I thought — Dr Anders? Myself? The man in the attic?

The machine on Mrs Washbourne's table began buzzing.

Mrs Washbourne went back to the table. She pressed a button and seemed to listen.

I thought — They are about to receive their instructions about what to do when the world is on fire?

Then — I must meet someone, sometime, with whom I can talk easily about how crazy all this is; without always having to remember how crazy I may be myself.

Mrs Washbourne said 'Yes?' and then 'Directly.'

She looked at Uncle Bill; then at me, then at the door.

Uncle Bill got up and went over to the machine on the table.

I thought — The bell has rung: orders are about to be given to the servants of Andromeda.

I got up and went to the door.

I thought — I am supposed to think that they can prevent what will happen to the world?

Uncle Bill was saying into the machine 'Yes': then 'Not very clearly.'

As I went into the hall I thought — Is it their unconscious they are talking to? That pursues them like wolves? That they think they can placate, from the back of their troika, by throwing out the world?

X

I said to Dr Anders —

'Look, is it any wonder that people don't make sense? How does anyone know what's going on? People with all the information don't know what's going on. There are all these impressions coming in and of course we have to filter them; to make up stories, obsessions; or how would life be possible? To take in everything we'd be gods; or mad. But because people can't see this, can't see themselves making up stories, they have to imagine they make up the whole: and this makes them mad; or sad; because they're always disappointed. Other bits of the whole, that is, are always coming in, to upset them. So even the stories they make up have to be mad or sad; to justify their disappointment.

'Can you think of any work of European literature or of any other literature for that matter that's not to do with life being a disappointment? That's not trying to comfort people by saying how awful other people's lives are? Oh I know — there are stories about animals, and fairy stories and suchlike; but what work trying to describe what human life's really like makes it out to be a successfully going concern? Something you'd be pleased to be part of? And yet it is, isn't it? Don't people want, after all, more to live than to die? Or at least with parts of themselves? Well this doesn't mean that all writers are fools or liars. It means that they're doing with language what language lets them do: with the limitations it imposes. Language is to do with protection; it's part of the system that filters what's coming in; it's suited to saying what things are not rather than what they are; it deals with disappointments. Even if people do know about life being a successfully going concern they can't easily talk about this; it doesn't sound right; language is to do with parts, with stories that have a beginning and a middle and an end, and parts are properly sad, because they have limits.

What is successful is to do with the whole.

'But what if people knew something about all this — I mean they do, but what if they tried to form some language about it — wouldn't the language they formed to try to describe how life might be a successfully going concern and thus about the whole, be a language not just of stories and obsessions but about our need to make up stories and obsessions and so a language to enable us to talk about this too; not just a filter but a way of looking at filters; to clean them even — I don't know about this — but at least some effort at the whole? Wouldn't it even be like psychoanalysis? We sit and lie here, and listen, and talk; and we talk what we talk about, and about the way we talk; and what gets understood happens mysteriously. But it is this that is the going concern: that is to do with the whole. And this we know, even if we can't talk about it directly. But I mean — insofar as we could get a language in which to talk about stories and filters as well as to tell stories in the manner of filters, then we would be getting a glimpse of the whole — and it would be this that would make us happy — there would be no disappointments — because when other bits came in, of the whole, this is what we would be interested in. From other people's filters. For you'd know they had these. They might even be interested in yours. Even make it easier for you to unblock them. I don't know about this. But what you would have glimpsed would have been something working. Even if it sometimes upset you. What might you learn from its upsetting you! Oh I know all this is difficult. This sort of language. I haven't got hold of it yet. But I shouldn't, should I? Isn't this what I'm saying? — Let it go.'

Then — 'That girl I told you about, do you think she'll be any good for me?'

Dr Anders had for some time appeared to be asleep.

I thought — What I am trying to say is, that the whole is known not by definition, but by a process of endeavour.

I said 'You know that bit in Plato where a person is always looking for his other half or twin. And those recognition scenes in Shakespeare where what has been lost is found, or what is dead comes alive — '

71

Dr Anders made a faint noise like a dog having a dream about hunting.

I said 'Well, all this depends on some sort of miracle. Which is the sense of the whole. Do you think, in fact, in the outside world, after one has made one's efforts, after one has tried to see one's stories, the fact that one feels better — and this is a fact — means that the whatever it is that flows through you, or happens to you, in the outside world, is something that provides miracles?'

Dr Anders looked up sharply and gazed out of the window.

She said 'Meaningful coincidences — '

I said 'Ah.'

Then — 'Or do you think it is just to do with the twenty-one lost chromosomes?'

She said 'What twenty-one lost chromosomes?'

I said 'You know that thing about everyone having forty-two chromosomes only half of which go on to the children — '

Dr Anders said 'Forty-six.'

I thought I might shout — All right, forty-six!

I said ' — So they have to spend their lives trying to find the other twenty-three again, or whatever it is, like Plato's lost half of a cell.'

Dr Anders said nothing.

I thought — Oh all right, my mother and my father then.

But — It is true this language is difficult!

I said 'There was a day when I was about seven or eight, I sup-pose, and we were living in London at the time, and I had had a quarrel with my sister. And I thought I was in the right, but my mother was disapproving of both of us equally. So I went and locked myself in a bathroom. To teach people how to treat me properly, I suppose. Like Napoleon. And I swore that I would not come out until justice had been done and seen to have been done to each of us equally. I mean Napoleon, I suppose, just wanted a lot of dignity. Our house in London was a tall house with three or four storeys. The bathroom I had locked myself into was on the third floor. I was quite good at locking myself in, I had done this before; I settled down with a bathmat and a towel on the floor and made a sort of bed with my head down by the lavatory. There was a good lock on the door: they would have to break it to get in. And I would rather starve than go out. You see how politics grows from family life, don't you. Children have such power over parents: parents feel guilty: though why they should I don't know, since children have such power. Well there I was, on the bathroom floor; and getting a bit hungry every now and then, with my head down by the lavatory. I thought it would be better if I starved, of course, because then my parents would feel guilty: but I wished I could either starve or not starve rather quickly, because otherwise things might get uncomfortable. Well my mother and sister came and banged on the door every now and then: they asked me to come out: they even offered me food. But I didn't come out, for what would then have been the point of locking myself in a lavatory? I had to be a sacrifice, like Napoleon. Well after a time my mother and sister left me alone: they weren't fools: perhaps they knew after all that armies don't have much power if they're left alone in an empty landscape. Well that was the hard time, with nothing happening. And I was hoping the air would hurry up and give out: so I could die and be carried out and comforted. And see the beneficial effects on my parents of my suicide. If I was alive, that is: if you believe in Shakespeare's miracles. You see, this language is not easy. After a time I began to wonder whether something more important might be happening outside: such as chocolate cake for tea, or other people coming to supper. In fact it was Aunt Mavis coming to supper: but that didn't seem to matter much either way. Oh I know it's all a bit more serious — or is it? — a child locked in a lavatory and thinking about dying: I was only seven or eight. What was my mother doing? Why didn't she break the door down: scream, yell? Was that what I was asking? How much did I know. Enough to know that if she had, I suppose, I would have thought of killing myself. Which was why she didn't? I wonder if I knew this. I was quite a clever little boy: for eight or seven. But what on earth, short of death, was to get me out of the lavatory? Death of one sort or another, of dignity and pride, or a real death, getting attention. Do you think my mother knew this? Well, what I am saying. You don't have to lose all pride: how does life go on? What are the ways of tapping that miracle? But that is the end of the story. Anyway, I had been there several hours — my mother and my sister had come back once or twice and had even pushed food under the door — some sort of half sandwich I think — and I had pushed it back again — it's not difficult to go on a hunger-strike when life is boring. Then pain becomes more interesting. But in this case, how could I ever come out of the lavatory? Then I heard my father come home. He had been out — where? — after one of his girls, I shouldn't wonder. But that's another story. And they were telling him this story — about my being locked in the lavatory. And with Aunt Mavis coming to dinner! Or how terrible if they were not even telling him! That would be worse than Napoleon alone in Moscow. Then I would surely have to die. Then I heard my father say "Get an axe." And I thought I would undoubtedly kill myself. But had I not blamed my mother earlier for not getting an axe? I was, wasn't I, not only a clever little boy, but also half-witted. But I'm not saying for parents it is easy. No. I thought I could climb out on the window and then appear to be about to fall — what would it be — some twenty feet onto some railings. And then they would feel guilty. In full view of the neighbours. But still, would I be there to see it? Then I heard my father say "No don't get an axe, let's take this chance to have a little peace and quiet." And I thought I should now undoubtedly have to die: for this was the final insult! That they should want peace and quiet! When I was in the lavatory! But then again, if they did not care, what was the point of killing myself? Ah, don't these knots make patterns! like figures of eight! like an hour-glass! It began to seem as if I might never get out of the lavatory. What I am saying is, of course, that children can't win: but can't parents? The house had become strangely quiet. They were all I suppose having dinner. I thought I should climb out of the window. And then disappear. And begin a new life I suppose in Australia. Well there was a ledge, and then a gap, and then the ledge of another window. And beyond this a drainpipe. And if I got to the second ledge, I thought I could reach this drainpipe. And then I could climb down and both die and not die, because I might come alive again like one of Shake-

74

speare's heroines in Australia. Or one of the twenty-three lost chromosomes. Having been found by a shepherd in a basket on a mountain. Or been seen walking in the garden. You see, there are things you can't say. Can you? Do you think the Holy Ghost was perching all the time on the shoulder of that good scarecrow? Well, where was I. Getting out on to the ledge of that window. I can't remember this part of it very well. I suppose I was very frightened. Perhaps it really was about twenty feet onto the spikes of some railings. I got as far as one knee and one hand on the ledge of the second window and then I got stuck. Oh why didn't you sweep me up into your arms my mother! And the sash of the window was stuck too. I was quite a brave little boy. I didn't panic. This was the position that I had put myself in — had put my parents in — wasn't it what I had wanted? So we get what we want. Don't we. But I had wanted something more complex. Then I heard my father in the courtyard below. He was saying something like — "Now hold on with your left hand till you've got a better hold with your right" — or — "Try to get that knee an inch or two closer than that to the drainpipe." That old know-all. Walking in the garden. Treating it as if it were a purely mechanical predicament. Which it was, partly. A way of getting out of it. To put it in a different context. How did he know? When he got out of that garden? My mother and sister and Aunt Mavis had come out into the courtyard and were saying things like — "Call the fire brigade!" — and my father was saying — "No, he's doing all right." And me stuck up on my tightrope and just about dying. And he was telling the others to go back into the house. Then I got one hand and one foot on to the drainpipe. It was not all that difficult. With someone else below me, and watching and talking. With language doing what it is good at: exorcising: and then something magical takes over. One's being able to fly, suddenly, like an arrow. Straight to the target. After one has done all the talking. Then I was climbing down the drainpipe. Or perhaps it was not anything like twenty feet to the railings below. My father was saying — "It's good to know that one can get down from the top floor if there's a fire." You see, this is the point of the story: to have got the whole thing out onto something different; where we could see ourselves; from another framework. And so not be trapped. And I was looking down at my knee that was slightly bleeding. You see, this was what I knew about Sheila when she was behind her bathroom door. One does pass on, in some way, doesn't one, acquired learning. And then we were going into the house, my father and I. And my father was saying — "The problem now of course is how ever again to get back into the lavatory." I said "You can push a piece of paper under the door and then work the key through so that it falls on the paper." My father said "That's brilliant." We were going up the stairs to the first floor. My father said "Do you think there's a big enough gap beneath the door?" I said "Yes, they tried to push through a sandwich." My father said "A whole sandwich?" I said "No, half a sandwich." We were by this time outside the sitting room on the first floor. My mother and my sister and Aunt Mavis were watching. They were like actors on the edge of a stage trying to look like the Eumenides. My father said "One of the odd things is, that people are absolutely brilliant at doing things like climbing down drainpipes and getting keys from the wrong sides of doors, but are absolutely hopeless at things like knowing what to do about their feelings." I said "Why is this?" My father said "There's some theory about the human brain being superimposed on a much older brain, of some mammal or even reptile or something, but I don't think that's very well authenticated." We were going on up the stairs to the bathroom. I said "Do you think things will get better?" He said "Oh I think so, don't you?" Then — "But I think it will depend on two things: one, the way the wind changes; and two, on a person's being in some sort of readiness to move in any of several ways when it does." '

Then, to Dr Anders, I said — 'Oh I know I'm quite like my parents, I like them, why shouldn't I? I'm even like my mother; who came in to see me that night and sat on the end of my bed as if she were a statue on the banks of the Nile; and onto whose shoulder I put my head and cried: and if she did not hold me quite as tightly as I would have liked then isn't this because she wants to respect people equally so that it will be the wind and not herself that will carry them when it does?'

XI

I was asked to go to a pop concert by Sally Rogers, the television personality.

When she rang up the telephone was answered by one of the secretaries in Cowley Street, and I had to talk in the hall. Mrs Washbourne came and listened to me and I had the impression of dozens of eyes watching me from behind portraits or two-way mirrors.

'Thank you very much!'

'You've got that. Time and place.'

'Thank you very much!'

I thought — One day I will get hold of that old man at my windpipe and I will stick him through his own throat like St George.

Sally Rogers was about ten years older than me. I thought — I am flattered: but isn't it true that the flatterers we so much like we also despise?

Then — But we still might be able to act the parts of Miss Paragon and the Belgian Schoolgirls.

The pop concert we were going to was in one of those enormous halls where people come from all around as if to witness some visitation. Word has got out that some children, or such-like, have seen the Virgin Mary on a plain in Spain or Portugal or somewhere; and so everybody rushes to jump on the band-wagon. They beat their arms around about them in the cold; thus frightening away, and with hot dogs and trinkets, the holy spirits that might otherwise have gathered.

When we were in our seats — Sally Rogers was wearing a T-shirt and jeans and looked peculiarly like my sister — she took my hand and put it beneath her thigh. I thought — Now I can put my other hand on top of her thigh and she can put her other thigh on top of that and we can play the children's game of slapping things one on top of the other until everything goes wild and you're banging about as if in an orgy.

The star at the pop concert was going to be Tammy Burns. Tammy Burns was a very beautiful boy rather like the boy I had been in love with at school. The point of homosexual love, I thought — Sally Rogers was squeezing my hand beneath her thigh and was gazing at me with the tip of her tongue between her teeth — is that one can do roughly what one likes; one does not have to worry too much about what is expected by the other person in the way of performance.

Sally Rogers said 'Exciting!'

I said 'Yes isn't it.'

She said 'You don't sound very excited.'

There had been a good deal of publicity about this series of concerts by Tammy Burns because he did, in fact, make some sort of appearance as the Virgin Mary. A plastic grotto had been built on the stage into which he emerged and stood almost naked — one hand over his breast and the other over his groin — while laser-beams played around him like a halo. Someone (perhaps himself?) had brought a prosecution against him for blasphemy; which of course had increased the popularity of his concerts enormously.

Sally Rogers said 'I've got a plan for afterwards!'

I said 'Oh what?'

She said 'I won't tell you.'

The plastic grotto, before the concert began, was shrouded in a sort of dust sheet: as if religious symbolism had been put away in moth balls.

I thought — But what of that bird that flew down between pillars; was it the bird that was first sent out of the ark?

In the first half of the concert there was a group with a xylophone and it was as if we were in the inside of an enormous bell. I thought — This is the line of men with guns; the noise that shoots birds down as they come back on that shaft of sunlight.

Sally Rogers said 'Afterwards we'll meet Tammy Burns!'

I said 'Oh will we?'

'Come on, come on, you ought to be saying — '

'But I am!'

78

She said ' — What is this old bitch up to, who wants to intro-
duce me to Tammy Burns? — '

I thought — Ah, I will like Sally Rogers.

When the second half of the programme began I could no
longer hear anything that Sally Rogers said. Her mouth opened
and shut and from time to time I put my ear down to it; and
once she put her tongue into my ear. I thought — Well, this is
the real thing, isn't it?

Then — At the tower of Babel, after that bird had gone,
wasn't it tongues that God confused so that men should not be
angels?

On the stage the dust sheet had begun to glow as if a huge
head were about to come through it.

I thought — But what was the language that men had before
Babel, that was making them like gods?

With Sally Rogers' tongue, there had been the feeling of a
snake getting into the apple of the world —

The dust sheet, glowing on the stage, was like a grub about
to burst into a butterfly.

I thought — What is the word for this — Imago?

Sally Rogers had taken out a pad of paper and a pencil and
was writing on it — *What would you like to do with Tammy
Burns?*

I took Sally Rogers' pencil and paper and I looked at it for a
while. Then I tried to draw a face using her writing as a skeleton
— her top words for hair, her lower words for eyes and mouth,
an oval enclosing them. It came out quite like Tammy Burns.

Sally Rogers took the drawing back and stared at it. She
turned it this way and that.

Then she put it between her thighs.

When Tammy Burns came on he emerged through the dust
sheet like a sort of baby: there he was, almost naked, with one
hand across his breast and another at his groin. (Or his grotto, I
might have said?) There were a lot of lights like blood around
him. He was grotesque. He was also beautiful. I do not know
how to write about this. I mean, he was in some way blas-
phemous. We have got used to the idea that things like images
of the Virgin Mary can be beautiful; that things like a parody of

79

the Virgin Mary can be clever or nasty but not beautiful; what we have not got used to is the idea that if we know now about these images, the power of them because they are inside us, then what better can we do perhaps than to smile at them as well as say they are beautiful? To take our projections back inside us; perhaps even teasingly; but also to love them; and for the same reason — that they are ours.

I wondered if I might be a bit in love with Tammy Burns.

The song that he sang was a slow, deep, drawling sort of thing that was called, I think, "Miss Skylight." It was all about some girl wanting to be rescued from — what — where she was trapped? In a grotto? A lavatory? A womb? Tammy Burns sang it in a deep growing voice as if he were trying to amuse or to reassure himself; that he was not, or was, really a girl that he loved; as if a record were being played at a speed different from that which it was made for. The accompanying music was rather quiet: with wispy bits like entrails. The point of the song was that it made a sort of commentary on the image and the music; on what had once been so beautiful; which had become corny perhaps but which now again might be beautiful; because someone was so painstakingly holding it up to be cared about; rather deprecatingly perhaps; but as if it were a good baby. I know I cannot write very well about this. Tammy Burns did have some sort of magic: which was to show that a really beautiful thing is what is beautiful anyway; but then there is the struggle to be able equally to accept it: to feel at home with it.

When Tammy Burns came down from his pedestal he tried to dance and as the show went on I thought he became rather embarrassing. But then — Did he not want to be embarrassing, because that is what something being born is anyway?

Then I thought — Is he not rather like that girl at Sally Rogers' party?

Then I became so involved in my thoughts about the bird that had gone out of the ark and had later slid down to a birth on a shaft of sunlight that I did not notice much of the rest of the concert.

Then, when we were out in the street and there were people

running rather deliberately this way and that as if there was a fire and they were animals looking for water Sally Rogers said —

'What would your uncle have made of that?'

I said 'What would my uncle have made of what?'

She said 'All right, all right, Mr Skylight!'

In Sally Rogers' small car we sat while people pushed round us as if they were a stream and we were an egg. I was thinking — Before Babel, would language have been music?

Sally Rogers said 'Do you think he's gay?'

I said 'My uncle?'

She said 'Tammy Burns!'

I thought — If we built a tower to the gods now, the language would not be music: we know too much: music is meaning separated from knowledge.

Sally Rogers' small car jerked forward as if it were having ejaculations.

The place to which we were going was some sort of club, or pub, where show-business people went in the evenings. Tammy Burns, Sally Rogers said, would come in later.

I thought — Will I be able to tell him that when he dances he should try to be not a girl but a bird?

The pub, or club, was a red-plush place with candelabra and mirrors. I thought I should try to get drunk as quickly as possible; then I could stop thinking and talk; could perhaps even become the life and soul of the party.

I was thinking — But the language would be silence; and our actions rather than our words would be like music.

I said 'Let me get the drinks.'

Sally Rogers said 'No, you're not a member.'

I said 'I can act as if I were a member.'

Sally Rogers said 'I'm sure you can.'

When she came back with a whole bottle of whisky I thought — Well, this is indeed all right: I can imagine myself as the Hall Porter in Miss Paragon and the Belgian Schoolgirls.

Then Sally Rogers said 'What's your uncle going to do about these strikes?'

I said 'Oh good heavens, I don't think he's going to do anything about the strikes!'

She said 'But is he or isn't he going to call in troops?'

I thought that I might say — No, he's going to call in the Libyans.

I said 'What else do you want to know about my uncle?'

She seemed to think about this for a time. She looked away round the red-plush landscape.

I said 'Do you want to know where he gets his money from?'

She said 'Well, where does he get his money from?'

I said 'The Liberals.'

She said 'Sorry — '

I said 'Is that why you asked me out?'

She said 'Did you think I asked you out for a quick fuck?'

The pub or club had a lot of glittering people in it; they were like models practising the poses they would be dug up in in a million years; to give evidence of social disintegration, before the ice-cap came down from the pole.

After a time I said 'I hoped so.'

She said 'Well then we'll have a quick fuck.'

I thought — Oh what am I going to do when I like Sally Rogers?

I said 'I'm sure my uncle doesn't know what he'll do about the strikes. But I think he's right that it's usually best for governments to do nothing.'

I could explain — Then people, surely, expend themselves?

I said 'And I don't know where he gets his money from, I don't think anywhere interesting, and it may not even be true that he spends more than he earns normally.'

Sally said 'You know that girl you had your eyes on at my party?'

I said 'Yes?'

She said 'She's called Judith Ponsonby.'

I thought — I am about to learn from Sally Rogers something that so far has been out of my reach.

Sally said 'She lives at 18 Ruskin Square.'

I thought — Good heavens! Then — That's very posh.

I said 'Thank you.' Then — 'The reason why I might not have seemed too friendly to you straight away, is that there's a terrible lot going on in my head, and you're quite like my sister.'

Sally said 'What's going on in your head besides Judith Ponsonby and your sister?'

I said 'I quite love my sister.'

She said 'Then get it out, get it out, Mr Avalanche.'

I thought — What good new names! Sally Rogers! Judith Ponsonby!

When Tammy Burns came in he was wearing a white overcoat down to his ankles. He was somewhat painted. He began to go round people greeting them like one of those grandmasters at chess who take on a roomful of amateurs: rather quickly, not saying much, with his eyes inside him: but everyone concentrating on him; getting close to him as if they might touch him but not quite; as if they did not want his strength too much to fly out of him. As he approached Sally and myself I wanted to find some move on my chess board that would be more than a game: more even than what I had been playing with Sally. But I saw Sally's eyes adoring him and I thought — Ah, she will spoil it! But then, how else could I have got to Tammy Burns? Then when he was quite close and Sally seemed ready to flatter him I thought — But what is that story of the Zen master who comes round his pupils and he carries a stick and he says — If you say I am holding this stick I will hit you with it and if you do not say I am holding this stick I will hit you with it — and his pupils do not know what to say: they are in awe of him, looking up at him so shiningly! Then when Tammy Burns was opposite me I knew that he was indeed like the boy I had been in love with at school: something hot and dry and dusty about the mouth and eyes: like an afternoon in some foreign city. Or like Judith Ponsonby. And I remembered that what the Zen pupil has to do if he wants to be free is to get up and snatch the stick from the master's hand and thus upset the whole chess board.

XII

When I got home very late that night or in the early hours of the morning I let myself into Cowley Street and I thought that this time at least no one except the policeman by the door would see me, and I went upstairs holding my shoes like people do in cartoons; but the door was open into Aunt Mavis' room and the light was on and there was a sort of scratching noise. I thought — Not that man again like President Nixon! In the room Aunt Mavis was on her hands and knees and she seemed to be pulling at the carpet. She wore a white nightdress and her bones showed through like those of an old horse. I thought — Or like the madonna fallen from her grotto; her plaster and wires in the dust.

Aunt Mavis said 'Come in and shut the door.'

I said 'I thought I heard a noise.'

Aunt Mavis said 'They've got this place bugged.'

She clambered upright. She went to the window and put a hand up against the wall. Her nightdress gaped at the side.

I thought — Or like some bird unable to fly, trying to get back into its cage again.

I said 'Is Uncle Bill here?'

She said 'He's with that woman.'

I thought — Surely he's been with Mrs Washbourne too long for Aunt Mavis to call her that woman?

I did not know what to do. I sometimes sat on the edge of Aunt Mavis' bed and chatted to her in the evenings.

I said 'Have they really got this house bugged?'

She said 'I think it's behind the shutters.'

I thought — Or is she like one of Goya's disasters of war?

I said 'But I mean, if you found wires, they'd probably just be false wires put in to make you find them. And the real wires would be somewhere different. Like burglar alarms. Or there wouldn't be any real wires, that's what they'd have wanted, to make you think they were real wires to save expenses. Or they might be real ones. Or anything.'

She said 'There was a man here the other day.'

I said 'Yes, did you see him?'

I thought — Am I as drunk as she is? Do I think the house is bugged?

Then she said 'They've got photographs.'

Aunt Mavis used to keep bottles of sherry in her room. Sometimes she called them cough-medicine. She would wait till someone was passing her open door, and then take a swig from her bottle.

I had thought — She wants to be rescued then?

Or now — She's forgotten where she's pretended to hide her bottle?

I thought I should go over and act as if I too were trying to find something behind the arras.

I said 'What sort of photographs?'

She said 'Look — '

There were in fact wires attached to the shutters. They were thin, and went down to a junction box near the floor. But I thought they must be to do with old burglar alarms which I knew were installed, but were seldom turned on.

Aunt Mavis said 'Go to that drawer.'

The burglar alarms were not turned on because Aunt Mavis used to set them off: and then when the police arrived it was difficult to explain about Aunt Mavis, either that she was drunk or that she was not.

'Which drawer?'

She said 'I'm not decent.' She giggled.

She sat on the edge of the bed and put her feet up.

I don't know if I've explained about Aunt Mavis. We used to see her quite a lot when we were children. We had a house in the country, and she used to come and stay there and play croquet. She would arrive with her own special mallet which had brass rings round the ends, and she would hit her balls very hard into the shrubbery. She and my sister would have terrible arguments about whether or not the shrubbery was out of bounds, and whether her balls could be replaced a mallet's length on to the lawn.

I went to one of Aunt Mavis' chests of drawers and opened a drawer and there were a lot of those soft women's clothes like packets of bacon.

She said 'One drawer down.'

I thought — What would Dr Anders say about my thinking that women's clothes are like packets of bacon?

Aunt Mavis said 'Underneath the jumpers.'

Once, when I had been a child, and we had been having supper with Aunt Mavis, she had taken her teeth out while sitting at the table and had held them in front of her face and moved them slightly as if she were a ventriloquist and she were having a conversation with her dummy.

She said 'Find it?'

It was after incidents like this at the supper table I think that Aunt Mavis had gone away to do a cure for alcoholics. My mother and father did not seem to talk about this much: as if they thought it both funny, and too tragic.

Underneath the jumpers, and skirts, and furs like bits of old skin (I thought — Is it that I am frightened of death? My mother's?) I came across a mounted photograph, about six inches by four, which I recognised as being one of those such as used to be taken in the thirties or forties on a seaside pier. I had seen illustrations of these in books. You put your head or heads through holes cut out of a piece of boarding from the back, and on the front were painted bodies in shapes and poses that made you look ridiculous. In this particular photograph the painted bodies were those of a very fat lady and a baby she was pushing in a pram. The heads, coming through the holes from the back and superimposed on the bodies, were those of Mrs Washbourne and Uncle Bill.

Aunt Mavis said 'You recognise them?'

I said 'Yes.'

I thought — Is she saying something very subtle here, which is that this is a bit of profound symbolism representing something true about Mrs Washbourne and Uncle Bill? or is she just being half-witted?

She said 'She's pushing him in a pram.'

I said 'I know.'

There are primitive tribes, I had read somewhere, who when they are shown a photograph are unable to make out what it is about: they turn it this way and that, as if it were a piece of paper with just a design on it, or perhaps as if it were the reality it is representing.

Aunt Mavis said 'It's that woman.'

I said 'Yes.'

Aunt Mavis put her arms round her knees and rocked to and fro.

I wondered — But might Mrs Washbourne and Uncle Bill in fact do something like this? I had read in one of my pornographic magazines of a man who liked to sit in a pram outside his house in some suburb —

Aunt Mavis suddenly put her head back and opened her mouth and made a noise like paper tearing.

I said 'But Aunt Mavis, this is painted on wood. You put your head through from the back. It was taken on a pier. It's the sort of thing people did, you know, when they wanted to cheer themselves up at the seaside. I expect it was taken at one of those political conferences, you know, where politicians must want to cheer themselves up.'

Aunt Mavis said 'It certainly is funny!'

Then she laughed again as if her inside was coming out.

I said 'Aunt Mavis come to bed.'

She leaned forward and gazed at me intently.

I thought — Anthropologists do no good by trying to explain things reasonably to strange tribes —

Aunt Mavis said 'He had an affair with your mother, did you know?'

I thought — You shouldn't say that!

Then — She is like someone in the electric chair.

I said 'Who did?'

She said 'Your uncle.'

I thought — O my prophetic soul! —

I said 'What do you mean affair?'

She said 'I just thought you should know.'

I thought — I bet you did!

Then — Act one, scene four or five; that old goat, that ghost, that smiling, damned villain —

She said 'I think it had quite a lot to do with the break-up of your father's and mother's marriage.'

I said 'What break-up?'

I thought — Oh what shall I do with you if I have no crucifixes, if I cannot fart at you? Put my fingers in your eyes and turn you inside out like an octopus?

After a time she said 'Oh don't tell me you don't know about your father's and mother's marriage!'

I said 'There's nothing broken about my father's and mother's marriage. They just don't see much of each other, that's all. There can be terrible and ridiculous things about marriages that go on all the time, can't there?'

She looked at me crookedly: then her whole face seemed to begin to fall sideways as if she were a tower with clouds rushing past her.

I said 'What sort of affair did they have? Was it a good affair, bad affair, sad affair, a happy affair? Who cares about affairs? What matters is whether or not people are killing and dying with envy and resentment.'

I thought — That old fool Hamlet should have stuck his mother up the arse as well as the arras.

Then — But Aunt Mavis is not my mother?

She rocked backwards and forwards as if she were someone acting crying. Then she put her head in her hands. She said 'I so adored your mother!'

I said 'I bet you did!'

I began to wonder how I could continue this scene more successfully than Hamlet. She was just an old woman: there might be bugging devices behind the arras.

Aunt Mavis said 'Oh Sophie! Sophie! Forgive me!'

I walked round the room. I thought — Oh my mother, my mother, you do what you like! And my father with those girls like snakes in the long grass —

Then — Who is it I want to kill? Uncle Bill? Myself?

Then — Good heavens, Dr Anders will have a field day!

As I walked round I wondered — Where is that fourth wall which actors like to think either is or is not there; to let them preen, as if in a mirror, their awful emotions?

I said 'When did my mother and Uncle Bill have an affair?'

She said 'In California.'

I said 'And what was Mrs Washbourne doing?'

Aunt Mavis took her hands away from her face. She looked quite sober. She said 'What do you mean, what was Nellie Washbourne doing?'

I thought — The point is, if we are our own audience, we could see all this is ridiculous.

I said ' — Pushing Uncle Bill in a pram?'

Aunt Mavis got off to bed. She came and took the photograph away from me briskly.

She said 'I thought you'd be interested!'

I thought — O Ophelia, Ophelia, can you not come quickly: can we not holds hands and run along a sea-shore that is not a painted back-drop on a pier —

Then — Actors, if they do not know that their audience is themselves, at least they know that they are acting?

Aunt Mavis put the photograph carefully back in the drawer.

I remembered — But when I used to go to the theatre with Sheila I wanted to shout — Come on, ref, break it up!

The whole performance in which Aunt Mavis and I had been involved — my coming into her room; her being on her hands and knees; the finding of the photograph of Uncle Bill and Mrs Washbourne; my wondering whether I should be reasonable; her telling me about Uncle Bill and my mother — all this seemed to be to do with an experiment about what is acting and what is not: what is behind the arras or a seaside pier: what is beyond the necessary framework of a stage; as we sit in the wings of our conscious or unconscious —

I thought — O Ophelia, let us go through streets where tanks are aiming their guns at this old barracks!

Aunt Mavis said 'Sh!' Then she stamped on the ground.

After a time there was a creak like a cat mewing.

She said 'You see?'

I thought — Where did I once think; witches have cats?

I said 'It sounds like a teddy-bear.'

Aunt Mavis went to her bed and climbed into it and pulled up the bedclothes to her chin.

She said 'What did you do tonight?'

I said 'Oh, nothing — '

I thought — But what if there were some demonstration by which people could know they had to act out perhaps all their ridiculous emotional dramas — somewhat formally perhaps — people bashing each other about, pulling each other's hair, fucking their own or each other's mothers — I mean we like these dramas — why else should we like to watch them? But at the same time we don't — I mean we don't like them — so, where was I — so that at the same time they wouldn't be trapped in them — the people — the actors — they'd be saying — Look! isn't this what you like? But also not — because, you see, this is what we're showing you — you can also get out — by getting all this stuff out — as if on to a stage —

I said 'I met Tammy Burns.'

Aunt Mavis said 'Did you have a good time with him?'

I said 'Yes, I did, really.'

She said 'Oh well that's good then.'

I said 'And what did you do?'

She said 'I wanted to be an actress.'

I said 'And what stopped you?'

She said 'I got stage fright.'

I said 'Couldn't you have given marvellous performances, if you had stage fright?'

She said 'No, I couldn't, it was too difficult, really.'

XIII

I said to Dr Anders —

'Well, what happened was that Tammy Burns ordered me a drink — I hadn't done very much: you don't have to do very much you know: I mean I think I know about these people; what else is the point of stammering? They don't like speaking much either. Or rather Tammy Burns told one of his hangers-on to get me a drink; or just nodded to him; he always has hangers-on, you know, I suppose to prevent other people pinching little bits off him. Well when this drink came there wasn't one for Sally Rogers. They were doing this on purpose I suppose: Tammy Burns was just standing around: it's his thing just to stand around: so people can watch him and want to pinch little bits; as if he isn't a human being but a thing: this is quite powerful you know: human beings get a sort of force around them, if you look at them as things. You want to see if you'd get a shock if you touched them. I was thinking about myself I suppose. I mean, I can stand around without talking longer than anyone. As if language were a sort of insulation. Well, Tammy Burns still hadn't said anything. He'd just ordered me a drink. So we were getting on rather well weren't we. And I was thinking — This sort of homosexual thing, you don't have to make anything, you don't have to prove anything, it's either there or it isn't: have I said this before? But after a time Sally Rogers had to say — Don't I get a drink? — because this wasn't her thing: silence: but then what was she doing there anyway? I mean she'd taken me to the club. And she had her own bottle of whisky. I do think that with women you have to be proving things, don't you? Or is this old-fashioned. I suppose you'll say — What women? There's only this or that woman. But don't other people find this? I'm joking! Well anyway. But it did seem as if I had to get a drink for Sally Rogers, or I had to get one of

Tammy Burns' hangers-on to get her a drink, or I wouldn't be doing my stuff as a sort of man for her. Isn't this awful? A man as a sort of dispensing machine; or juke-box. But if I spoke, I wouldn't be doing my stuff for Tammy Burns: as a sort of spook I mean. So I was trapped! Grow up! But what else was the point of the evening? Of course I wanted to get off with Tammy Burns. But to have dumped Sally Rogers wouldn't have been spook either, you see. And he was rather like the boy I had an affair with at school. All this was like a ballet. How could I move! except by some signs, or signals. So I just raised my glass, as if it were a test-tube or something, and stared at it, and waited, as if to see if there were angels or bubbles or something: if you cut out language, you see, what happens if you wait? Then after a time Tammy Burns did nod to one of his hangers-on; and the hanger-on went to get Sally Rogers a drink.

'Well then when the time came to leave the pub or club — do you think this is unbearable? or do you think this was the sort of thing that was happening in the Tower of Babel before God sent languages? — when the time came for us to leave the club or pub all this happened again: this drama! this clash of armies! Well, isn't it better if it's funny? I mean, one of Tammy Burns' hangers-on came up to me and said would I like to go back to some house they were all going to in North London or somewhere; and he didn't say anything else I mean: nothing about Sally. And you don't think it's anything to do with my being a nephew of the Prime Minister, do you? because I don't; what would Tammy Burns do with the nephew of a Prime Minister? Except to send him an autograph, perhaps, if it was paid for. Well anyway. There was all this happening again. And Sally Rogers had to say — Don't I come too? Because she still wasn't used to this. The spook stuff. Though she was quite a star herself I suppose. Or do you think in heterosexual things you can't wait: you have to talk: you have to have food for your baby? What do I mean by this? You can't talk music. Well anyway, where was I: outside that club or pub. What do you think I meant by getting food; and not being able to talk music?'

Dr Anders said nothing.

I said — 'Well, I was a bit fed up by this time. And a bit drunk too I suppose. So I thought — What if I do something sensational! like speak to Tammy Burns! a move in a chess game that has never been thought of before! except once by Capablanca in 1920. So I went up to Tammy Burns and said — "Can Sally come too?" As if I were snatching the stick out of that Zen master's hand and giving him a whack with it — '

I thought — Is it this that I will one day have to do with Dr Anders?

I said — 'So Sally and I got into his car, it was an enormous car, like you think those sort of people cannot really have but do, a car with darkened windows and little fold-out seats and we were all piled on top of each other as if we were in a telephone box; there were so many people there to stop people touching Tammy Burns; and I was on one of the little seats in the middle facing front with Sally on my knees; and Tammy Burns was behind me. And someone began stroking my hair. I suppose it was Tammy Burns. And Sally was putting my hand on her breast. All such powerful people! And I thought — But what have I to protect myself against: this is the opposite of stammering — '

I felt the white light coming down again across my heart, my mind.

There was Dr Anders' bookcase, her frieze, the spire beyond her window.

I said — 'Well anyway, we got to this house, I don't know whose, an enormous house in North London: with sort of Moorish architecture, you know, with tiles and things like a lavatory. Or a brothel. I mean I suppose like a brothel; in some film about the eighteen nineties in Paris or Munich. Well anyway. And in fact there was a film going on in the house all the time: along one wall in the sitting room: like a gigantic cinema screen; for all these people who don't speak much, who have to have images, who try to turn themselves into things. And people weren't paying much attention to the film; were even occasionally moving to and fro in front of it — '

I thought suddenly — Like Plato's cave?

Then — I must remember this.

I said ' — And all the people, in the half dark, sitting about, were Tammy Burns' henchmen; and they were like primitive cave-men, yes; with this projection of their unconscious. And the film they were watching, or not watching, was a pornographic film: it went on all the time: it was in the background of their minds: but by showing it on the wall did they recognise this; did they make it any better? It was one of those films, you know, of huge arseholes and cunts and penises: boring away all the time: in the half dark, with people watching and not watching it: half moving about in front of it: like life: or was it? People just getting up to fetch drinks and snacks and things: and then settling down again: all these things in their minds, but because it was on the wall could they turn away from it? Get it out. Get it out. But it had also half killed them. They were sitting around, as I sometimes do, listening; to — what — music?'

I thought — For God's sake, what is it I have against music?

I said 'Or like gas that comes in through little pipes in the ceiling — '

I thought — Oh come on, you can think and talk like music!

I said — 'Well anyway, Sally Rogers had sat down with a few others facing the wall. Do you think this was like Plato's cave? Watching breasts and cunts and penises? In their unconscious? But then, what was the reality, and the sun, outside. I went into a sort of alcove. I mean it was three o'clock in the morning. We were in this house in North London. With all this stuff on the wall. And I did not really want to look at it. But also of course I did. We do have these memories. But there was this alcove, with a fountain and lights; as if I could be a sort of Narcissus. I mean, I wanted to find out something about myself: about survival. In this difficult world. To live in it, with it; not to be beaten. By all this lunacy. Do you know those old plays where there are a courtyard and a fountain and a loggia? And a tree. And a moon. I mean this was a sort of stock stage-set. For people to remember things by. Remember what they really were, and not be beaten. So I thought — I will sit here and then perhaps something will happen against this other backdrop of my mind: such as a girl with long hair letting it down like a rope

94

from a balcony; or that bird which came into a courtyard sliding on a shaft of sunlight — '

I thought — Why do I say it cannot be talked about?

Dr Anders made a small sound as if she might be snoring.

I said — 'Well, Tammy Burns came into the alcove. I was sitting on the parapet of the fountain looking down into the water. Or rather, Tammy Burns didn't quite come in; he stood by the door; so that his profile was against the images projected on the wall of the sitting room behind. All the cunts and arseholes and penises. And children, you know: dear God, this is not easy! Nor are wars, revolutions. Tammy Burns stood there with his back against the pillar: as if he were part of the stage-set: his profile cutting into the stuff on the wall behind: framing it: as if, by moving, he might appear to make it move; like a train being left by a station. And I thought I could say to him — Listen, what is it that you know? I mean, in that grotto: when you are like the Virgin Mary? And he came and sat beside me on the parapet of the fountain. He said "What do you want to do?" I said "Make a film." He said "What sort of film?" I said "One that will be a sort of frame that one might move slightly in and out of as if it were one's conscious and unconscious." Our two faces were in the water which, if we kept still, remained quite clear. He said "How can you do that?" He put out a hand and touched the water. His face, his real face, shivered. I said "When you get down from that grotto, you should act, or dance, as if you were being made love to and were a bird." '

After a time Dr Anders said 'The perfect rapport.'

I thought — How vulgar!

Dr Anders said 'Unlike you and Sally Rogers.'

I said 'I haven't told you yet about me and Sally Rogers!'

Dr Anders put her arms on the sides of her chair — her signal that the session was nearly over.

I said 'I haven't even told you about Aunt Mavis!'

She said 'But you didn't stay with him.'

I said 'No.'

I wanted to ask — What is it do you think I have been trying to tell you?

Dr Anders got up from her chair. She went to the door. She

said 'You were more interested in the experiment.'

I thought — The experiment of whether or not anyone understands me?

Then she said 'I thought you were going to tell me about whether your uncle's house was being bugged.'

I said 'I can't really stay interested in all that.'

Then I thought — Can't I really not stay interested in Uncle Bill and my mother?

— All those old breasts and cunts and penises —

I said 'You know what you once told me about the language of love — '

She said 'What did I tell you?'

She stood with her hand on the door.

I said 'I had been talking one day and you said — But that isn't the language of love! — and I said — What is? — and you didn't say anything for a time; and then you made your sort of cooing noise, or mewing, as if you were holding a baby.'

Dr Anders waited with her hand on the door.

I said 'I haven't even told you about my mother.'

She said 'You haven't even shown me your stammer.'

XIV

I thought I should go and sit in the gardens of the square where Judith Ponsonby lived: which I had been told about by Sally Rogers.

I held some sort of conversation with myself about why I wanted to sit in the square rather than to find out Judith Ponsonby's telephone number and ring her up. I said — But if you pursue people, you do not know if it's really them you want to get; you just know you want the pursuit. And I answered — But isn't it this that you were saying about homosexual rather than heterosexual love: that in the latter there has to be performance, and so there has to be pursuit?

The gardens of the square had railings round them and notices saying Residents Only. I climbed over the railings and I sat on a bench beside some bushes where I could observe the front door of Judith Ponsonby's house.

I said to myself — All right, if you just let things happen then it is like homosexual love because it is like loving yourself: but if you have to make things happen, which is like heterosexual love, then still, you would have to sit back sometimes and observe whether what seems to be happening is true, or how would you know that you were not chasing yourself?

Judith Ponsonby's door had white pillars and a portico. I was uneasy about her living in such a grand house. I thought — But is not all loving the hope of starting from, then going on from, where one is oneself?

There were children playing on the grass. They had foreign girls as nursemaids. The girls were like hens waiting to peck at the children and then deposit them on the ground again like shit.

I was not really waiting for Judith Ponsonby: I was waiting to see whether or not she would come out. In fact, if she came out, would I hide in the bushes?

I thought — I am like a body frightened of being taken over by a visitor from Andromeda.

I was suddenly not even sure if I had got the right house. I had not made a note of what Sally Rogers had said. But then — Did this matter, if what I was interested in was not Judith Ponsonby, but seeing whether or not she came out?

The nursemaids were gobbling amongst themselves like turkeys. From time to time they would make a dash at the children, as if to pick off bits of fluff for their nests.

I thought I should try to write something in my notebook. There was a mystery here about these images of hens and turkeys, for I imagined birds to be symbols of something divine.

I found a blank page in my notebook. I blew on it.

After a time a man's voice said 'Are you a resident?'

I said 'No.'

'Get off then.'

The man wore thick boots like torn-up tree stumps.

I wondered if I should say — I'm MI5.

What I had written in my notebook was — The person one loved should be involved in the same experiment.

'Did you hear what I said?'

I said 'I'm MI5.'

The man was wearing a peaked cap. He had a thin face and a small moustache like Hitler.

I had thought — Birds peck at the mind; for good or bad; the experiment would be, to find when good or bad could equally be useful.

I said 'I'm waiting for someone.'

He said 'Who.'

I said 'Judith Ponsonby.'

I wanted to write down — With someone one loved, one could watch life hand in hand, and good and bad would be like a culture growing.

He said 'Where does she live?'

'Number 18.'

'She doesn't live at number 18.'

I had a terrible urge to pick the man up and throw him into the bushes.

He put his hand into his breast pocket.

I thought — In films, would he be going to pull out a pistol?

I was afraid I was losing what I had been about to write down.

The man pulled out what looked like a police whistle.

I snatched his whistle and hurled it into the bushes.

He got down on his hands and knees to go after it.

I thought — I could put my foot against his behind and push him further in —

Then — What is this violence, that even on hands and knees there is confusion about whether he is a persecutor or a victim?

I began to walk across the grass. It was such a bright day. The nursemaids were in rows. I wondered — Is it true, that victims are people who summon violence with police whistles?

Then — Wars usually start at the end of a long summer.

I wondered if the man in the peaked cap was coming after me.

When I was out in the street — I had gone through a gate, I had not bothered to vault the railings — there was the traffic and the people on the pavement as if taken over by Andromeda. Nowadays there was no war; so placards made up stories about warfare. If one asked people what they were doing, how many would say — Staying alive?

There was a placard by a man selling newspapers which said *PM Hits Miners.*

I saw Judith Ponsonby coming towards me on the pavement.

I at first did not recognise her. I had been thinking of going back to the man in the peaked cap and saying — Sorry, but it is people like you who start wars; who make other people so awful; not because you are violent, but because you are victims. But I did not think I could make him understand this.

Then there was this girl coming towards me. For a moment she was like the goddess Andromeda herself being pulled along by her sea-monster. Then I recognised Judith Ponsonby.

She wore a short leather skirt and had strong legs. She was pulled by a dog on a lead.

I was so amazed that I stepped into the road and a man ran into me on a bicycle.

I said 'Sorry.'

The man said 'I might have been killed!'

Judith Ponsonby was going past me on the pavement. The man I had knocked off his bicycle had fair crinkly hair. I thought — But he is not, is he, the man who was in the attic of Uncle Bill's house like President Nixon?

Judith Ponsonby had stopped just past me. Her dog was peeing against a lamp-post. I thought — That is her dark horse, to take her to her beloved.

I said to the man with crinkly hair 'You wouldn't have been killed because you ran into me: you'd only have been killed if you'd swerved out into the traffic.'

He said 'Aren't I lucky then.'

I thought this was quite witty.

Judith Ponsonby had raised a hand and was looking across the road as if for a taxi.

The man with crinkly hair said 'I'm Jake Weatherby.'

Judith Ponsonby was one of those smooth, perfectly rounded girls who are like stones in the shape of eggs: or a dancer in an American musical which, like herself, would be booked up for ever.

I stretched a hand out across the road as if to help Judith Ponsonby get a taxi. In doing this, I knocked again against Jake Weatherby.

He said 'I say!'

Then the man in the peaked cap came rushing out of the gardens with his whistle.

Jake Weatherby said 'Can I have a word with you?'

The man in the peaked cap blew his whistle.

There was a taxi on the other side of the road.

The taxi-driver, hearing the whistle and seeing me with my arm raised, swung across the road and pulled up in front of Judith Ponsonby.

Judith Ponsonby, who had been watching me, said 'That's brilliant!'

The man in the peaked cap, having seen me turn towards

him with my arm raised, turned and ran back into the garden.

I opened the door of the taxi.

Jake Weatherby said 'What's up?'

Judith Ponsonby said 'I could always do with someone like you!'

She climbed into the taxi.

She had boots halfway up her thighs: above them, sun-spots like explosions.

When she was in the taxi she smiled at me. I waved.

Jake Weatherby said 'I know quite a good place round here.'

The taxi moved away.

I turned and went with Jake Weatherby.

I thought — But I am mad to let her go!

Then — He is not that flat-faced homosexual?

Jake Weatherby said 'You keep turning round. Is there any-one following you?'

I said 'Yes, a man in a peaked cap with a whistle.'

I thought — I did not even hear where the taxi was taking her!

I tried to remember exactly what had happened. She had seen me reach out my hand; then there had been the whistle; then the taxi had drawn up. She had said — That's brilliant! Then — I could always do with someone like you!

Jake Weatherby said 'It was lucky I spotted you.'

Then when the taxi had drawn away, she had smiled and I had waved at her.

Jake Weatherby said 'What shall I do with my bike?'

The point was, it was as if she and I had always known one another.

I said 'Can't you chain it to the railings?'

We had come to a pub.

And when she climbed into the taxi, there had been those tongues like flames coming down —

Jake Weatherby said 'You do know who I am, don't you?'

I thought — But I do know where she lives, don't I?

Inside the pub Jake Weatherby went to get beer. I sat with my back against a wall. I thought — It would have been useless if I had pursued her.

Then — But there is evidence, is there not, that she is the person with whom, for me, good and bad might be the same?

I tried to work out who Jake Weatherby was. He wasn't the man in the attic, because he had fair hair. He wasn't the flat-faced homosexual, because he was younger. He wasn't the man in white overalls, because he wasn't like the famous actor. Nor, I thought, was he one of Tammy Burns' henchmen, although he was buying me a drink. So was he one of the people put on to follow me by Uncle Bill? Or a gossip column person such as Aunt Mavis got things from? Or was he just some devil or angel sent to bump into me so that when I first spoke to Judith Ponsonby things would appear magical; and chariots of fire would come down?

Jake Weatherby came back with two glasses of beer. He said 'Do you mind if I talk to you?'

I thought — And it was in fact practical, even if I let her go, that some pattern was set up of things being magical —

He said 'About your uncle.'

I said 'Yes.'

He said 'You know there are these stories.'

I could say to Dr Anders — But are they, these coincidences — these men with whistles and men on bicycles and dogs which drag girls along to pee on lamp-posts — are they or are they not in the outside as well as in the inside world?

He said 'You may be able to help me.'

I though I should try to concentrate very hard on what this man was saying, in order not to float off like a balloon.

There were some men at the bar who were watching us closely. I realised I was still wearing Uncle Bill's bedroom slippers.

Jake Weatherby said 'There are some photographs.'

I said 'What photographs.'

He said 'I think, stolen.'

I thought — But coincidences can be part of the law of averages?

Jake Weatherby was looking round the pub carefully.

Then he said 'Ave Maria! The Mafia! The whole bloody shooting match!'

I thought — Ave Maria? The Mafia? Uncle Bill's whole shooting match?

Then — One picks what one wants to pick from these averages —

Jake Weatherby pulled out a piece of paper and began writing on it.

I thought — Like Sally Rogers at the pop concert; will he now push some message in my ear?

Jake Weatherby held out the piece of paper to me. He had written — *We can't talk here. I think we are being overheard.*

I wondered — Am I supposed to take this piece of paper and screw it up and swallow it?

There were all these people in the pub with flat, expressionless faces: like men outside pornographic bookshops.

Jake Weatherby took back the paper and wrote — *May I get in touch with you?*

I took his piece of paper and held it.

I said 'Yes.'

I folded the piece of paper into a dart. I launched it across the pub.

Jake Weatherby seemed about to go after it; as if to prevent it from falling into the wrong hands.

XV

One day I went to the country to see my sister, who is called Lilia. She lived in Suffolk, in a cottage, with a man much older than herself. I had not met this man. He was another of the things that my mother and father did not much talk about: not, I think, because he was so much older than my sister, but because they could use this as an excuse not to have to talk about something about which there was not much to be said anyway.

My sister is quite a few years older than I. We had been close to each other as children.

I sometimes think that my sister and I are the opposites of the people who come from the same egg and are always trying to find one another again: we seem always to be trying to get away, but it is with each other that we feel at home.

My sister met me at the railway station. We sat in her small car while she tried to get it into reverse. Then after a time she said 'Could you walk ahead of me on the pavement please with a red flag or something?'

When she drove she leaned close to the steering-wheel and stared ahead as if her dark eyes might be a cow-catcher to pick up people and deposit them on the sidewalk.

I said 'How much do you remember of our childhood?'

She said 'Not much.'

I thought — I will not, if I'm good, will I, tell her about what Aunt Mavis said about our mother and Uncle Bill?

I said 'I'm going to this Dr Anders you know.'

When we got to her cottage there were rambling roses and honeysuckle over the porch and the whole thing seemed to be the setting for an opera. I thought — Will her elderly lover appear and sing for ten minutes in knee breeches?

She said 'I don't think it matters, do you, if we don't

remember much about childhood. I think we have to get new parents anyway as we go along.'

I wanted to say — But I remember about you: you remember about me?

I said 'This is like the cottage in *La Traviata.*'

She said 'It is not like the cottage in *La Traviata!*'

I said 'What about your young brother coming like that old father, you know, and singing for ten minutes about how you're ruining the family reputation?'

She said 'I'm not going to die!'

All I knew about her lover was, that he was some sort of professor.

When she got out of the car she seemed to be rather over-dressed for this time of year; with a heavy leather waistcoat and gumboots.

I thought — You mean, you're thinking you may die?

I said 'Why didn't she just tell him, that old father, in the opera, to go and chase himself?'

She said 'Dear brother, you're always chasing yourself.'

I thought — That's witty.

I wandered through into the sitting room. I looked for signs like pipes and tobacco and burnt holes in cushions.

I said 'How is the Prof?'

She said 'Don't call him the Prof!'

Then — 'He's quite all right thank you.'

I said 'No one ever asks me how Sheila is; just because she's not glamorous.'

She said 'I was just going to ask you about that, tiny boots.'

This was from a joke we had had in my childhood; when everyone used to tell me I was too big for my boots.

I said 'Well as a matter of fact Sheila and I have broken up. That's why I've come down to see you, to cry one of those heartbroken arias.'

She said 'And I thought you'd come to see me because you're jealous that it's me who's ruining the family reputation.'

My sister looked good when she was doing things like stand-ing in front of a stove and cooking; because you didn't expect someone so pretty to be good at banging pots and pans about.

She said 'And how is Dr Anders?'

I said 'Do you know, the extraordinary thing is, when I talk to her, it all comes pouring out.'

She said 'Dear cloaca maxima, when has it ever not come pouring out?'

I thought — Her Professor teaches her the classics?

Then — Do we talk like this because in family love you are having neither to do what you want nor to make anything, but are simply at home?

I said 'Have you noticed, my sister, that every now and then, I stammer?'

She was keeping her back to me at the cooker. She was wearing this leather jerkin. I thought — Is she pregnant?

She said 'Nevertheless, brother, whenever has it not come pouring out, except when you want to be insufferably silent and spooky, in order to torture your nearest and dearest, such as your sister.'

I thought — Do, or do not, brothers imagine that their sisters are pregnant?

I said 'This thing about getting new parents. Do you think one has enough genes, from long ago, to be able to choose, a bit, what sort of parents, or suchlike, with whom one wants to grow?'

She said 'I don't know, do you?'

I thought I might say — Can you ask the Professor?

She was cooking lunch. She always stood rather wide-legged; sturdy. As if she were cultivating children.

I thought — Is this where I would like to be at home? with a girl in a kitchen banging about and doing things for me?

I said 'Would the Prof know about that?'

She shouted 'Don't call him the Prof!'

Then — 'I expect he does; I'll ask him.'

She brought over plates, cutlery, dishes. She was a very good cook.

I said 'Do you know a girl called Judith Ponsonby?'

She said 'No, are you in love with her?'

I said 'I think love's overrated, don't you?'

She said 'What would you put in its place?'

I said 'Respect. What's seemly.'

She put roast beef in front of me. I thought — Good cooking is the doing of simple things well: it is the doing that is so complicated?

She said 'Tell me if it's underdone.'

I said 'It's not underdone.'

She said 'Seemly!'

Then she came over and put her cheek against mine.

I wondered — Why don't I ask, Are you pregnant?

— Might she be having a bad time with the Professor?

We sat opposite each other and ate roast beef that was like flowers.

I said 'I am jealous.'

'Who of.'

'Him.'

She suddenly began to cry.

The table was between us. I thought — No, I do not get up and put an arm around you.

I said 'Are you pregnant?'

She said 'Yes.'

I said 'I thought you might be.'

She said 'Well why didn't you say so.'

I said 'I did.'

Then — 'It might not have been seemly.'

I thought — What happened, Lilia, when that bird came down between pillars?

I said 'Well that's good.'

She said 'Good!'

I did not think she would worry too much about not being married. She was clever at things like being in a cottage with honeysuckle and roses.

I said 'You're not getting married?'

She said 'No.'

I thought I could say — Well, that's all right then.

She said 'It's not his baby.'

I said 'Oh I see.'

I thought — What do I see?

— A pond, with a duck on it —

She said 'At least, I think it isn't.'

I tried to work this out. It was not the Professor's baby, but it was him she was going to stay with? So. We went on eating. I thought — Shovelling food into one's open mouth like possibilities —

I said 'Whose is it then?'

She said 'I wanted to get rid of it.'

I said 'Why?'

She said 'Oh why, why!'

I went on eating. I thought — You mean, you also didn't want to get rid of it?

I said 'What stopped you?'

I thought — That Holy Ghost, on its shaft of sunlight?

She got up and took some plates and bashed them about in the sink with her back to me.

I said 'Why shouldn't it have two fathers? The Holy Ghost had two fathers. They fought a whole war about this in the fourth century or something. This has always seemed to me to be one of the few sensible things people have fought a war about, not whether the Holy Ghost had this father or that, but whether or not it had two.'

She said 'And who won?'

I said 'The people who said it had two, I imagine.'

She said 'Well they weren't having the baby.'

She came back to me with some treacle pudding.

I tried to concentrate on this. I could say — But none of this matters: there's that bird on a window-ledge: it is you, is it not, who will be having your baby?

She said 'As a matter of fact, it was you who stopped me.'

I thought — I stopped you?

Then — Getting rid of it?

So — Is this when the bright light comes down; the drop onto some railings —

She said 'Do you want to hear?'

I said 'Yes.'

I thought — Here, there are these connections?

She lit a cigarette, which she did not usually do. She backed away as if the smoke were coming after her.

108

She said 'Well I had gone to one of those clinics, you know — '

I thought — She should not smoke because of the baby?

She said ' — Oh God it was so awful!'

She was sitting in profile to me across the table.

She said 'I had to wait. This was just at the time when you might be going to Dr Anders. I remembered I'd promised to telephone Dr Anders — '

I thought — You telephone Dr Anders?

She said ' — to talk about you.'

I said 'You know Dr Anders?'

I could not understand this. I thought — You didn't tell me?

She pulled the smoke from her cigarette in, blew it out, tried to move her head away; as if a cloth were being held to her face by torturers.

She said 'And then, when I was talking to Dr Anders from this call box in this awful place, you know, this clinic; and I was telling her about you — '

I thought — But of course I might have known that you knew Dr Anders!

' — She then said, on the telephone — You talk about him as if he were your child.'

Lilia began to cry properly now; her whole face dissolving.

I said 'Your child.'

She said 'Yes.'

I thought — And the baby is alive.

Then she shouted, through her tears, 'Oh of course I know Dr Anders! Who do you think it was who put you on to Dr Anders!'

I said 'I didn't know.'

I had always thought it must have been my parents, or Uncle Bill, or Aunt Mavis —

I thought — So indeed, who are my parents?

She said 'And then when I was talking to Dr Anders on the telephone I remembered that time when you were by that drainpipe on that awful window-ledge and I had prayed so hard you wouldn't die!'

She was crying terribly now. I thought I would cry too.

She said 'It would have been so awful if you had died!'

I thought — And somewhere, on some stage-set, singers in honour of us are doing something like *La Traviata* —

— And on a stage-set no one dies?

She was making so much noise crying that she was like an orchestra drowning the voices.

I got up and came round the table and put an arm round her. I said 'Hey, no one's died!'

Then I wondered — Will it be like me, that baby?

I held out a handkerchief. It seemed to have a lot of ink on it.

She blew her nose. Then she said 'Doesn't Sheila wash your handkerchiefs?'

I thought I could save a joke till later — No, she's only interested in brainwashing.

Then my sister said 'Anyway, I walked out of that awful place. And so now I've got this baby. And please can I wash this handkerchief.'

I said 'Yes.'

We sat for a time in a sort of stupor. I thought — But still, things go on busily, underneath, like ants in trees —

— But also what is it, in humans, that produces seeds; that are carried away in the wind?

She said 'When will you be going up to Cambridge?'

I said 'I'm not going to Cambridge.'

She said 'Oh no, you're going to Dr Anders.'

I thought — Her Professor is at Cambridge?

Then — Might it have been he who put her on to Dr Anders?

I said 'Who's the other father, the real one, or the one you think it might be, then?'

She said 'You don't know him.'

I thought — Would he look like a bird sitting in a tree?

I said 'Do you love him?'

She said 'Oh love, love, what did you say — isn't it more important to be seemly?'

I said 'Isn't he?'

She said 'Oh is he seemly!'

She sometimes had a violence in her; like a tree struck by lightning.

I said 'Then what's wrong?'

She said 'Oh you'd sort everyone out, wouldn't you, oh I do love you!'

She put her head again against mine.

I said 'He's married — ?'

'Not now.'

'What then?'

'He's with some third-rate film-star.'

Some light in mind came on for a moment: then went out.

'But that's not the point.'

I said 'What is the point?'

She said 'I've told him I don't want him.'

'Why?'

She shouted again 'Oh why!'

I thought I could tell her — But if it is true that there are these coincidences in the outside world — my being on that drainpipe; your telephoning Dr Anders from the place where you went to get rid of your baby —

She said 'What's the point of breaking up a life and the other one's too?'

I thought — The other one's? Then — Yes, I see.

I said 'It would break up the Professor's?' Then — 'He thinks it's his?'

She said 'I don't know.'

Then — 'We're carrying on as if it is.'

I said again 'Why?'

She made as if to shout: then she said quietly 'Oh yes, why.'

She stood up and stretched. She walked round the room. She seemed to be showing off her baby.

I said 'Isn't the Prof seemly?'

She said 'Oh he's seemly! God, we're all so seemly!'

I said 'Then that's all right.'

I waited for a time. I wondered — What on earth was that image that came into my head a moment ago, and then fell out?

I said 'He'd mind if it wasn't his? How do you know?'

She put her head against the pane of a window, looking out.

I said 'Do you know, truly, who is the father?'

She said 'Maybe.'

I said 'It is the other one.'

She said nothing.

I thought — Of course, if she does or does not want change, there are still things that can't be said.

Then I said 'But don't you think he knows too?'

She seemed to think about this. Then she said 'The Prof?'

I said 'Well — '

She said 'But not the other — '

I said 'Well, could he?'

I could explain — We know, or don't know, what we want, or don't want, to know, don't we?

Then — But sometimes we learn what it is we want to know?

She said — 'You think I should tell him?'

'Who?'

'Both.' Then — 'Or just the other.'

I said 'Well, sooner or later, you can't do anything else, truly, can you.'

She said 'Which is what?'

I said 'There are all these angels flying about.'

She said 'You'll be even more insufferable, won't you.'

XVI

I said to Dr Anders —

'There was a day, I was about ten or eleven I suppose, and we were in the country — there was this house my mother and father rented to make out we were country people I imagine — and my father used to go out shooting rabbits with a .22 rifle — oh all right, I'll be stopping soon sniping at my father and my mother! — and of course I wanted to go out shooting too. So one afternoon when I thought they were all asleep — it was summer and they had had a big lunch and there were the sort of people staying you know who went to bed in the afternoons — I'm sorry! — I took the rifle from where my father had hidden it — it was a small rifle, you know, such as you shoot at targets with — and I thought I'd go to a pond at the bottom of the garden where ducks or moorhens sometimes came out and I'd wait there till an aeroplane flew over — the house was near some sort of training aerodrome and planes flew over quite often — and then I'd fire the rifle at a duck or moorhen or something and the noise would be drowned by the noise of the aeroplane overhead. And if I didn't hit the duck, the bullet would go into the water; and so I wouldn't do any harm. I knew how to work the rifle; one gets these things from television; also from my father. So I waited by the pond while moorhens came out; and then there was an aeroplane. I aimed at the water and fired and there was hardly any kick from the gun and I could see the rings on the water and one or two moorhens flying away. And I thought — Well, I've done it: now I can go back and hide the rifle. Then there was an exclamation or something from the far side of the pond; and my father sat up in some long grass. There was a sort of orchard at the far side of the pond: oh God, you don't think this is all too symbolic do you? How can I get away from it? There are often orchards at

113

the far side of ponds, aren't there? Well anyway, my father sat up, and he had his shirt off; he seemed to have been sunbathing. I thought he was in the house. Then he said something like — "Keep your head down"; and I thought at first he was talking to me. But there was someone beside him in the long grass. And I was trying to get the rifle out of sight behind a willow. And my father was putting up a hand and touching the trunk of the apple tree just above his head; as if a bullet had gone in there. But this it couldn't have done, I thought, because I'd fired at the water and seen the rings going out. But there did seem to be some newly made mark on the tree. Oh God, I suppose, or at that cross-roads! And then my mother was coming out of the house. And my father was putting his shirt on. And there was someone else sitting up in the long grass. It was a girl who had been staying the weekend; some actress, I suppose. And she was putting her shirt on. Anyway my mother was saying something like — "What on earth are you doing?" and it was as if she should be talking to me: but she was talking to my father. And my father was saying "Sunbathing." And he was saying it in that funny voice, you know, by which he made everything seem witty. And my mother was saying "There was a shot." And my father was saying "Almost bang on target." And all the time there was this girl. But they were paying no attention to me; though they were suggesting, you see, I had almost shot my father. Which was not funny, especially after — what? — he had not been so bad to me? I wanted to explain — That mark on the apple tree couldn't possibly have been me! I saw the rings go out on the water! But I had no chance; they were being witty. My mother said "What target?" My father said "The old cock robin." Then he began laughing. I wanted to explain that if any bullet had gone into the tree, it must have been from the aeroplane that had flown over. But this was absurd. Then my mother said "Where did you get that gun?" She was at last talking to me. But I couldn't think of anything witty. The girl in the long grass began crawling away. My father watched her. Then I did manage to say "My bullet went into the water." My father said "Bullets bounce off water." I said "Bullets don't bounce off water, they're heavier than water." And I was so much hating this. But what better could my father and mother have done? did I want them to punish me so that then I could have said — It's you who've been caught in the orchard! My father said "They can bounce off water if they're fired at a certain angle." My mother said "Need we go into this." My father said "As Oedipus said on his way to get the carving knife." I mean, I don't know if he said exactly this; but something like it. Would it have been better if they had poured out their anxiety over me? Screamed and shouted? Which is what most parents would have done. And of course, bullets can bounce off water. Then my mother said "At least if it had been Oedipus he'd have been caught with me." And my father had to lie down in the grass again because he was laughing so much. My mother was quite witty too, you see. And strong. I don't think that particular girl came to our house again. But what was it I minded? That I wouldn't be like them? Couldn't? Did I tell you, my aunt told me, that she — I mean my mother — had had an affair with my uncle?'

Dr Anders said nothing.

That white light not quite there this time; over my heart, my mind.

I thought — There are these feelings; did I think I had lost them?

I said 'But I don't really think I care about all that.'

I thought — I do know I am like my father and my mother? Also — They were, in fact, quite good to me.

— All those people in the auditorium settling down in their seats again —

I said 'I've lost it.'

Dr Anders said 'Lost what.'

I thought — Who needs a thread, when all the walls are tumbling down —

Then — It would, of course, have been easier to have been punished.

— So that now I would not have this freedom! This responsibility!

— I would not stammer?

That white light in the bathroom: my head down by the tiles.

I thought — But if I am like them, can I not now move on from them?

Then — Never again will I rather be a victim!

I said ' — That thread through the maze. The walls have fallen down.'

I waited for a time.

Then I said 'How do you think I ought to go on? Should I say I'm sorry?'

Dr Anders said 'Good God what for!'

I said 'Jokes, perhaps, are a sort of responsibility?'

Dr Anders pursed her lips. She looked out from the ledge of her mountain as if over an irrigated world.

She said 'Your mother did not ever really leave your father?'

I said 'Oh, there's another joke I remember. As my father watched the girl crawling away in the long grass, he said — "Saved from a fate worse than having to do all this for the kiddies." '

I thought — Now what did that mean?

Then — There's still a maze with mirrors?

Dr Anders said 'I think a child still wants to be given some-thing more.'

I thought — More than jokes? More than social work in California?

I said 'What.'

She said 'Something a bit humdrum.'

I thought — That they can feel superior to? Be at home in?

Then — Humdrum: a humming-bird —

I said 'But they need freedom too.'

She said 'Of course.'

I thought — Well, that's that; as we come back to a beginning.

Then — One day, we will pass on acquired learning?

I said 'My sister's having a baby.'

Dr Anders said nothing.

I wondered — Why did I say that?

I said 'I didn't know you knew my sister.'

I wondered — Is it the sign of an analysis doing its job, when there seems to be nothing more for an analyst to say?

I said 'But I must get away.'

116

Dr Anders said 'Get away from what?'

I thought — From minding that I am like my father and my mother; that they did not clamp their arms around me?

Then — That child of my sister's, will there be arms around it —

— To let it, or let it not, breathe?

I said 'Perhaps I have got away.'

Dr Anders said 'All this happens very early.'

I said 'What.'

She said 'Before you can really remember.'

Lying in Dr Anders' room, I found myself suddenly trying to see what was written on some papers on her desk.

I thought — I am learning, am I not, that there are things like networks that are better than arms to be put round people?

Then I thought I should explain to Dr Anders — Oh but I don't want to get away from you!

I had been thinking, I suppose, about getting away from Aunt Mavis and Uncle Bill and Mrs Washbourne.

I said 'But these things that start early, stop following you?'

Then there was this image of my sister having her baby.

Dr Anders said 'Where do you want to go?'

I said 'Oh, anywhere.'

— Where that light is by a fire; in my mind; and not just on a couch, or bedsprings, for an hour looking out of a window —

I was still trying to make out the writing on a paper on Dr Anders' desk.

Dr Anders said 'I think I should tell you that I shall be away all next week.'

I said 'Oh will you.'

She said 'Monday to Friday. At a conference. But I'll leave a number where you can get hold of me if you want to.'

I thought — You think I will be so lost without you, that I will die?

Then — Ah, but haven't I made images of a father and mother now to look after me —

I said 'I'll be all right.'

I wondered if I should say — What is your conference then?

Then I said 'I never knew it was my sister who put me on to you.'

Dr Anders said 'No?'

I wanted to say — Is your conference at Cambridge?

There was a letter on Dr Anders' desk with an address that I could not quite decipher.

I wondered — Will there always now be this profusion in my head and in my heart?

I said — 'That night I was with Sally Rogers, you know, after we had been with Tammy Burns: well, when we got back to her flat and there had been all those pornographic films, you know: well, Sally sort of took off her clothes like people do in films — dramatically, you know, like someone casting shadows — and then she was naked on the bed like Achilles in her golden armour. And she had one of those funny instruments beside her bed you know — like an electric tooth-brush or a humming-bird with its wings torn off — that are supposed to give you the most tremendous orgasms you know. Well, I didn't really want to do anything with this: I was very drunk you see: and the poor thing seemed quite dead. But Sally was getting nowhere playing with me, either, and was saying "This little piggy went to market." And I was saying "I'm afraid it's more like this little piggy's staying at home." And after a time I got up and went to the window and I held the vibrator in my hand. And I opened the window. And Sally said "What are you going to do?" And I said "See if it will fly." And I said to it — "Come along, coop, coop — " ' '

Dr Anders said 'And did it?'

I said 'Is your conference in Cambridge?'

XVII

On one of the afternoons during the week when Dr Anders was away I went to the House of Commons to see Uncle Bill perform. This was part of my effort to take the outside world of giants and politicians seriously: to see what life was like at the top of the beanstalk.

I stood in a queue outside the Houses of Parliament and tried to look inconspicuous. I seemed a head taller than any-one else. If I sagged at the knees and lowered my head I thought I might look like one of the Burghers of Calais in Roden's sculpture round the corner: and by thus seeming a victim, become one of the crowd.

There was an enormous hoarding to one side of where I stood on which someone had placed a small sticker which said *Oedipus loves Mary.*

I thought — Well, we have not done too badly, have we, my mother.

Then one of Uncle Bill's aides was passing by and saw me. At least, I think it was one of Uncle Bill's aides. I ran quickly through my list of — The man with crinkly hair; the man in white overalls; Jake Weatherby; the flat-faced homosexual —

'What are you doing here?'

'Waiting to get in.'

'Why didn't you let me know? I'd have got you a ticket.'

He led me out of the queue. I thought it would be too dif-ficult to explain — But I wanted to stand in the queue to find out what it was like not just to see Uncle Bill, but to be one of the people who queue up all night to get up the beanstalk.

We went through corridors and up in a lift and into one of those galleries where you sit and hang over the edge and wonder about dropping food down into the bear-pit below. There were all these men and women who looked absolutely at home there; as if they had found their ecological niche and would not change for millions of years. I thought — But this is the opposite of a zoo; where animals know they are on show, and so are uneasy. Here, they are so settled that if you dropped bread to them they would have you arrested for throwing stones.

— Sprawled about in those precise positions in which they would be when the lava came down: asleep, or dreaming of a world in which speeches came out clicking like the legs of chorus-girls —

I thought I would have to write this in my notebook.

There was a man talking about how if certain people got more money the economy would collapse: then another man was saying that if these people did not get more money the economy would collapse. The crowd seemed satisfied by this: to and fro, as in a tennis match.

Uncle Bill did not seem to have come in yet. There were men with their feet up on a table like barricades.

I thought — But do these people know how odd they are? Like flies caught in amber —

— Or are there always, so long as there is life, fingers that reach up like wild flowers out of gratings —

I found it hard to concentrate on what was being said. — Do not take this body of figures in one way: let us take this corpus in another. We have come both to bury Caesar and to praise him. Speech was being used like music or gas to come through little pipes in the ceiling: so that these old bones should not tell too much when they were dug up after thousands of years —

I thought — But can one save one's mind simply by ceasing to listen?

I was ruminating upon all this: thinking — Well, I seem anyway to have no choice; my mind is unable to dwell on such things: I mean the shot in Uncle Bill's study; the papers that Mrs Washbourne was or was not throwing into the fire; the photographs that might or might not have been stolen. From this sort of lava, like a hungry lion, good Lord deliver me —

— When there was a whispering noise to one side of me in the gallery and I saw trying to push towards me along the row of seats —

— Another of Uncle Bill's aides? The man like President Nixon?

It looked like Jake Weatherby.

I thought — But don't be taken in by this —

He had got some way along the row and was smiling and grimacing at me: then he had to sit down on the only seat available.

I thought — Please God, always take away the extra seat as in musical chairs; so there will be no room for these phantoms to get at me —

Down below Uncle Bill was coming in. He had his hands in his pockets with his thumbs pointing forward as if he were cannoning off invisible objects like a seaman. I thought — Politicians are sticks that we drop into a river; they go with the stream; then we rush to the other side of the bridge to see who is winning —

The man in the gallery was Jake Weatherby. He still seemed to be trying to attract my attention. I could say — But I am just getting the secrets of this strange tribe —

Uncle Bill had sat down and had put his feet up on the table.

I thought — They are the fossils that God put into the rocks in order to make us think he did not exist —

Jake Weatherby seemed to be trying to make people move so he could approach a few seats nearer to me.

From the back, a man wearing knee-breeches was frowning at him intently.

Down below there was a man saying — Now let us — what? — praise famous men —

I thought — Is Jake Weatherby my dark horse? My hungry lion?

Uncle Bill had sat up and was shuffling through some papers.

I thought — But the problem is still just how to stay alive.

There were all these fingers coming up through gratings —

I thought — I must be kind to myself.

The man with knee-breeches had come down and was talking to Jake Weatherby.

I stood up and began pushing along the row of seats in the

121

opposite direction.

Uncle Bill had stood up and had put on his spectacles. Then there was his bright, funny voice that seemed to be saying — Upsadaisy! With a glass of water and a parasol on a high wire. With a little skip, and a jump, like a child with a hoop. Then his hoop bowling out into the traffic?

I had pushed my way to the end of the gallery.

— I was the child running after the hoop: the hoop was the world —

I hoped that Jake Weatherby would be arrested by the man in knee-breeches, and so would not follow me.

I was banging down a staircase.

I wanted to say — Sorry! Sorry!

Though — Was it really a chance mutation that sent the world out bowling into this traffic —

When I was in the air I began hurrying towards Embankment Gardens. I wanted to look at Rodin's statue of the Burghers of Calais. Six old men, trapped in chains, whom everyone thought so beautiful —

I thought — Dear God, how could we stay alive if you did not send down your shit like lava on the world; or like manure —

A voice behind me said 'Hey!' It was Jake Weatherby.

I thought — I will now turn and take this man by the windpipe —

He said 'I must talk to you.'

I said 'All right.'

He said 'It's about your uncle.'

I said 'Yes.'

We were both standing by the statue: I was looking at Jake Weatherby; he was looking at the statue.

I thought — Is this it, now, why these old men are so beautiful: did we taste chains, Jake Weatherby, inside our mothers —

Jake Weatherby said 'They've got something on your uncle.'

I said 'What.'

He said 'What is it about this statue?'

It was such a grey cold day. With the wind beginning to gather leaves for the bonfire.

I said "If there's something unbearable about the subject

matter, you comfort it in the form.'

He said 'Of what.'

I began to walk towards the river.

He followed me.

I said 'What have they got on my uncle?'

He said 'Look, if I knew — ' Then — 'Documents. Photographs.'

I said 'Anyway who are they?'

We had come to the parapet of the embankment above the river. I tried again to face him. He kept turning away; as if he were a lion in a zoo.

I climbed on to the parapet above the river. The top was a narrow ledge a few inches wide. The river was a long way below. I held my arms out.

Jake Weatherby said 'What are you doing?'

I said 'Practising.'

He said 'For what?'

I walked along the parapet while Jake Weatherby moved along below me. I thought — I am a bird: if there is a tree, I will climb into its branches.

I said 'For when the ice-cap comes down from the pole.'

He said 'Are you trying to kill yourself?'

I said 'No, I'm trying to stay alive.'

The drop on the far side of the parapet was to mud. There were oil drums and old branches of trees there.

Jake Weatherby said 'I don't know who or what it is.'

I said 'Then why say it.'

He said 'Something about money.'

I had come to the branch of a tree. It stretched across the parapet. It seemed that I would have either to climb it, or to come down.

I said 'Is there anything else you have to tell me?'

He said 'I really wanted to pick your brains — '

I thought — I will slide down on that shaft of sunlight —

— Like a bird on a tea-tray —

On the ground, beside a bench, at the place where people rested in their walks beside the river, I had noticed an evening paper blown by the wind. On its front page, slightly muddied, there was a picture of a man lying on his back with what seemed to be a gag in his mouth. Above the picture was a huge headline — *Perhaia Slain.*

I climbed down from the parapet. I picked up the newspaper.

Mr Perhaia had been such a nice, quiet man. He had been found in the boot of a car, with a rope round his neck.

Jake Weatherby said 'You may be able to help your uncle.'

I said 'How.'

The photograph of Mr Perhaia did have something wrong about the mouth.

Jake Weatherby said 'There are people putting pressure on him.'

I said 'Dear God!'

The newspaper said that Mr Perhaia's body had been mutilated.

I put the newspaper back on the ground.

I thought — O bury him beneath the tree —

Jake Weatherby said 'They cut the poor bugger's balls off.'

I was going towards the road.

I said again 'Is there anything else you want to tell or to ask me?'

He said 'I can't talk to you like this.'

I said 'How can you talk to me?'

I thought — Oh damn, damn, what can I do for Mr Perhaia?

He said 'Where are you going?'

I was going towards where the traffic ran thickly. It was like molecules of gas that other molecules might or might not get through.

I thought — Run, run —

I said 'To the Tate Gallery.'

He said 'Why?'

I said 'To look at the people who are balancing on wires and jumping through hoops.'

He said 'You know, you're in trouble; can I help you?'

I dodged through the traffic. He stayed behind.

I thought — Molecules are like sea-gulls: they peck at you; some of you do, and some do not, get through.

XVIII

I rang up Sheila. I said 'Sheila, for God's sake, what have you told Brian Alick?'

Sheila said 'What do you mean, what have I told Brian Alick?'

I said 'I told you some joke. About my uncle getting money from the Libyans.'

She said 'I thought you said it was the Liberals.'

'That was a joke too. You were doing that thing about pretending to get something out of me — '

Then I thought — But was it not Sally Rogers that I said the thing to about the Liberals?

However — Does any of this matter, if language has broken down?

Sheila said 'Look, I can't talk about it now.'

I said 'Have you got that man with you?'

'Which man?'

I said 'The one in a white burnous like a Liberal — '

She rang off.

I stood in the call box.

I thought — But if one made enough jokes might one not keep the world on course as if with little jets when the bomb goes off?

I rang up Sally Rogers. I said 'Sally, you know I told you some joke about my Uncle Bill getting money from the Liberals — '

She said 'I heard you said it was the Libyans.'

I thought I might say — On a dark night, can you tell the difference?

She said 'As a matter of fact it's your Trotskyite friends who get money from the Libyans.'

I could not think of what to say to this —

— Oh I see! —

Or — Aren't the Trotskyites your friends then?

Sally said 'When are you coming to see me?'

I said 'I don't know. There's a man in a burnous on a bicycle following me.'

She said 'Well mind you don't end up like Perhaia.'

I rang off.

I was in a call box near Westminster Cathedral.

I thought — Well, I did try to be serious, didn't I?

Then — But where are those seeds growing, from what is buried beneath the tree —

I picked the receiver up again. I thought — Dial any old number and listen, and one would hear more sense than I get from Sheila or Sally Rogers —

There were a lot of loud clicks against my ear and then a booming noise as if pipes in a basement were having trouble.

I put the receiver down.

I thought — There are people sitting in underground cells in California who have worked out all the telephone codes and they can send messages round the world just by making clicking noises and blowing whistles —

— So, could not someone clever enough, witty enough, get himself plugged in to where he wanted and say what he wanted and then —

— as if with little jets —

— alter the world —

Could I put this into a film?

I banged the coin box of the telephone to see if any money might come out.

I thought — Once in a million million: those are fair chances, aren't they?

I needed money if I was to go on a journey.

I went out of the call box. I thought I might drop in on Sheila. I wanted to make love. I needed some bearings, before my journey.

I could explain to Dr Anders — But it is not sophisticated people who are witty: it is Cockneys and Jews and black people —

Then — Do I really mean that they are not sophisticated in trying to save the world?

I found I had not got enough money even to go by underground to Sheila's house.

I thought I would walk; and bang on coin boxes every now and then to lessen the chances.

For how else do we live; these people who make jokes; and try to keep the world on course? Ask the wolf in at the door? And he will not come, because we are not privileged?

It was such a cold day. I thought — The summer is over, when I was fed by Dr Anders and then made love to Sheila.

I found that I did miss Dr Anders when she was away. There was an ache in my head, heart, balls; as if something were being born there.

I thought — I will make love to Sheila again: then for a while this burden of thinking will be aborted —

— We are wandering Jews? Flying Dutchmen? This élite of non-privileged people?

— If I looked under the lids of dustbins, would I find a genie in a bottle —

— Or should I sing and dance, and pass my head round on a platter —

— When it rains it rains —

Occasionally I did an entrechat.

I thought — But you would have to keep things secret, wouldn't you, all you non-privileged people: or else the privileged would want to take away from you even the non-privileges that you have —

There were people on the pavement who did not pay much attention to me, or indeed to anyone who did not seem to come from Andromeda.

I thought — Being on the trail of meaning is so embarrassing!

When I got to Sheila's house there was the entryphone on her door and a little button with her name beside it as if she had gone up one rung on the social ladder and was now a prostitute.

The door was not locked; so I pushed and went in.

I thought I might say — I'm MI5. I'm MC^2 —

Sheila was not in her room. There were the two bed-frames on the floor. I thought — From these breasts I once used to hang.

I began to move around the room looking on Sheila's shelves and in cardboard boxes. I thought — It is now clear in my mind that people do this because they can't think of anything else —

Underneath some stockings, in one of her cardboard boxes, I found the three or four letters that I had written to Sheila. They were rolled in a cylinder with an elastic band around them.

I took the letters and sat down on the bed.

I thought — But if there really were this man, underground, plugged in to all the communication systems of the world; what, after he had made his clicks and his whistles, would be his message?

I read — *A revolution to be permanent would have to be aesthetic.*

I thought — Well that's all right isn't it?

Then — Did I get that from my father or my mother?

I heard footsteps on the stairs. I put the letters in my pocket.

I thought — I don't want them to pinch my message.

When Sheila came in it was as if she were not surprised to see me. I could not understand this. Then she acted as if she had suddenly remembered she ought to be surprised.

She said 'Look, I've got to talk to you.'

I said 'Yes everyone tells me that.'

She said 'What do you know about the Libyans.'

I said 'Nothing.' Then — 'Sheila, what on earth does it matter if you get money from the Libyans?'

She said 'Why do you say that?'

I said 'Libyans was just something that came into my head.'

She said 'Have you told anyone?'

I said 'No.'

She said 'Has anyone followed you here?'

I thought I could say — Sheila, Sheila, we once used to go and collect sea-shells on the beach where Blake saw visions —

Or — Yes, as a matter of fact, I was followed by a small fat man like a film director —

I said — 'I don't know if anyone followed me. And I don't know why things come into my head. Except it's interesting what does seem to have a counterpart in the outside world — '

Sheila went out of the room, slamming the door.

I thought that now I could lie back on the bed and read my letters.

I began to have some nostalgia about Sheila. She had been a girl with smooth shiny skin; her waterline protected from torpedoes —

I read — *Only what is aesthetic contains revolutions within itself.*

I thought — Well —

Then — But Sheila's footsteps went upstairs, not down.

I put my letters back in my pocket. I got up and opened the door. I went out quietly onto the landing. I looked up.

I thought — From an upstairs room she could have seen me arriving; and so not have seemed surprised?

There were faint voices coming from upstairs. One of them was a man's and the other might have been Sheila's.

I thought — She has been living up there all the time with that man like the famous actor?

I put my hand round my throat and made a strangling noise.

I thought — But this is not my message to the world!

I might kick against the banisters and say — Plasterboard! Plywood!

I went down the stairs making a banging noise. I could explain — A heavy body is being dragged down! I am being kidnapped!

I thought — It is true, I'm not upset —

— And I don't mind if this is condescending.

In the street there was an enormous dustcart going past with its mouth open at the back like a dragon's arse. I wanted to make a noise like a wolf, following it.

Then I crossed the street and went down a small alley between two houses opposite. I thought that from here I could watch the front of Sheila's house; to see what would happen, or who would come out.

I thought — Libyans! Liberals! These privileged people are not witty —

Then — Phantoms are what are dropped by dustmen out of dragons' arses.

While I was watching the front of Sheila's house a boy on a skateboard came whizzing down the road and as he passed the dustcart he swerved so that a car that was going the other way nearly ran over him. The man in the car yelled and the boy banged on the bonnet of the car and then the car pulled away with a backfire and a screech of tyres.

I thought — What, no pistol shot? No secret-service man like President Nixon?

Then — I must ask Dr Anders —

There was the street again quiet and mysterious as a film set.

I was half hidden behind a fence down the alley-way opposite Sheila's house.

I wanted to get an answer from Dr Anders about whether or not in the outside world —

A window on the second floor of Sheila's house opened and Sheila looked out.

Beside her was a man.

I had been thinking — There are these connections?

The man was Brian Alick.

I thought — Then it is he who has been living with her upstairs all the time?

— And the man in white overalls, when he did, or did not, go to make a telephone call —

— Yes, I see.

— What do I see?

A cat came and rubbed itself against my legs.

I thought — This cat, that is like a teddy-bear, once belonged to witches —

Then — It doesn't matter, here, what I do not see —

Sheila's head disappeared from the window.

I thought — Now, in a film, there would be something old-fashioned like a nun with a pram and jackboots showing beneath her habit —

— So, in the outside world, you make up things to look sinister when you fear that nothing is happening?

After a time the front door of Sheila's house opened and Sheila and Brian Alick half came out. They looked up and down the street carefully. Then they seemed to shelter again behind the front door of the house.

I thought — They are like targets at a fun-fair?

Sheila and Brian Alick appeared again. They ran to a small car

130

parked in the road. Brian Alick climbed into the driving seat: Sheila got in beside him. They drove away, fast.

I thought — That is all then?

I came out of the alley and began the journey back towards Cowley Street.

I tried to concentrate on the film I would one day make: in which things would happen as they did in fact happen; as if at random, but you have to make up patterns to live or to die —

But if you make them, who are you, there have to be patterns? You can't make, if they are you, you can only find?

Then — Why did the people in Plato's cave not come out into the sun —

— Was it because there was some old Zen master standing behind them with his stick and saying — If you say I am holding the sun I will hit you with it and if you do not say I am holding the sun I will hit you with it —

XIX

When I got back to Cowley Street I tried as usual to get upstairs without being seen. I seemed to be obsessed about this. I thought — Soon I must stay out for good; or I will be a bird caught by those old cats of witches.

I was caught by Mrs Washbourne on the first-floor landing. She said 'Can I have that jersey?'

I thought I might say — It's the only one I've got.

Or — You want my cloak of invisibility too?

She said 'You're invited to dinner.'

I said 'Oh am I?'

Going on up the stairs I worked out — She wanted to wash my jersey.

On the second-floor landing I was caught by Aunt Mavis. She said 'You didn't give that woman your jersey?'

In my room I sat and wondered what would happen if someone said just — I want to wash that jersey. Would there be the sound of trumpets: the walls fall down?

On the few occasions when I had had dinner with Uncle Bill and Aunt Mavis when there had been other people there I had sat halfway down the table and had managed to put off being spoken to by smiling and nodding as if I were either already playing a full part in the conversation or insane.

My father's old brown suit seemed to have grown a green mould on it. I wondered — How would one know if it were penicillin?

When I got down to the drawing room there was a man whom I recognised as an MP who appeared on television, and another man whom Uncle Bill introduced as The Editor. This made him sound like a racing correspondent.

There were also two women who remained separate from the men, and for whom I seemed to have been brought in like a eunuch.

One said 'You know Sally Rogers?'

I said 'Yes.'

She said 'Didn't you meet Tammy Burns?'

The men had gone into a corner and were talking amongst themselves. Or rather, the two strangers were talking but not really with Uncle Bill. They looked at him from time to time; but messages did not seem quite to be getting through from Andromeda.

I thought — The suitcases under his eyes are about to burst open like wounds.

The other woman said 'Do tell me, what's it like with Tammy Burns?'

I said 'I think he has the most terrible contempt for people.'

She said 'How exciting!'

I said 'Yes I think he's sad because he knows that too.'

When we went into dinner I saw again how exhausted Uncle Bill was. The suitcases under his eyes were like baboons' arses.

The first woman said 'Isn't he gay?'

The other woman said 'Isn't he a bit of liquorice all sorts?'

I thought — My efforts at communication, like Uncle Bill's, have been cut off to Andromeda.

I sat beside one woman: the other sat opposite. The Editor and the television MP talked at each other across the table. They were each side of Aunt Mavis. They were careful not to look too closely at Aunt Mavis. I thought — If she takes her teeth out and holds them up in front of her mouth, will they pretend she's eating lobster?

Then — But monks or monkeys, like myself and Uncle Bill — are they any better who do not talk at all?

I thought — Perhaps I should just watch out for what indicators or dials flicker to show whether people are still alive —

'She was a Moslem — '

'She was a Catholic — '

'She can't have been — '

'She was his mistress?'

'She was his wife.'

The television MP was a thin, rather delicate man with red

133

hair. The Editor was a thickset man with spectacles.

'Moslems don't always have two wives — '

'Catholics don't always have one — '

'Isn't that what I'm saying?'

'Perhaia?'

I was trying to memorise this conversation so that I might afterwards write it down. But it was difficult to get a hold of randomness without some memory-system, or rhyme.

The woman next to me was listening with shining eyes. I thought — As if to Hector and Achilles bashing away at each other with balls and chains —

'Who's got the money?'

'Who's got the child — '

'The hand that rocks the derrick — '

I did not think I could be getting this correctly.

I wondered how much I should drink. If I drank too little, I might never be able to talk again. But if I drank too much, I would not be able to talk either.

'Do you know the story of the woman who rushed at Perhaia with a bottle?'

This was Uncle Bill. I thought — Perhaps he has got drunk, in some effort not to talk at all.

'No?'

'He said — I'm sorry I only drink water.'

I thought — Aunt Mavis is doing quite well, just sitting there like a tower appearing to topple over with clouds rushing past her.

The television MP said 'You mean, the woman was going to hit him with the bottle?'

I thought that on the whole I should drink quite a lot: then, if the old Zen Master came behind me with his stick I could pretend I had meant to upset the table —

There were two decanters of wine. By filling up the glasses of the people on either side of me I could manage myself to get double rations in the middle.

Then Uncle Bill said 'Bert, here, has been hob-nobbing with the Trotskyites.'

I thought — Oh God, but have you forgotten I am the eunuch?

The television MP said 'Oh which ones?'

The Editor said 'Is there any difference?'

The television MP said — 'On a dark night — '

He was a rather fine-drawn man with kind eyes, and he sat with his hands under his legs and rocked backwards and forwards slightly.

I thought — He is like one of those small green parrots?

The Editor said 'It seems to me their programme is entirely destructive.'

I thought — O Aunt Mavis, take your teeth out!

One of the women said 'Yes I do find that depressing.'

I said 'They've got a feeling — '

Uncle Bill's eyes were so misty they were like the pearls of that dead sea-captain.

'A feeling? — '

'Yes — '

'Well that's something!' This was the Editor.

There was laughter.

I thought — But you are not someone who is supposed to laugh when I stammer!

Then — Let the flood come down —

I said ' — A feeling that things are so trivial in this society, so rotten, that what good can any programme do except be destructive? It's the sort of feeling, or the programme I suppose, that God must have had at the time of Noah.'

I thought — Bye bye to you on the land, you old fossils.

The Editor said 'And you call that constructive?'

I said 'Isn't God constructive?'

The Editor said 'Let's leave God out of this.'

Uncle Bill said 'He's a Catholic.'

I said 'Naturally.'

I got a laugh at this.

I thought — Dear God, I want to beat them, not join them.

The Editor said 'What's wrong with this society?'

I said 'It's not just that the wrong people have got money and power, which the Trotskyites say it is: it's that the people who do have money and power are so hopeless at doing anything except destroying themselves.'

The Editor said 'Destroying themselves?'

I said 'What skill it must take for reasonable people to appear so depressing!'

I wondered — Is he in fact the Editor of the *Farmer and Stockbreeder?*

I said 'People in this society wouldn't know what to do with themselves if things went well. They'd just dash around till they found something horrible again.'

I was trying to remember — What was it that happened to Noah when he was drunk? One of his sons saw him naked?

The two women had gone back to their food. I thought — What does all this mean — that in survival, people are simply embarrassing?

The Editor said 'And you think Marxists want things to go well?'

I said 'Yes, but they don't see that things are funny too.'

The television MP said 'Don't we?'

I said 'Perhaps, but we don't see the other thing.'

Then Uncle Bill said 'Bert, will you help your Aunt Mavis please?'

For some time I had half been aware of Aunt Mavis doing something like trying to pull her dress down over her wrists. This had seemed to be like making herself ready for the deluge.

I remembered how my mother and father had told me the story of how Aunt Mavis had come down one day without any clothes on to the lobby of a hotel. She had been caught by the doorman and turned round and put back into the lift.

Uncle Bill said 'Take the ladies upstairs for a while. We'll stay and watch it down here.'

He was referring, I supposed, to the television set which had been wheeled into the dining-room from the study.

I thought — They will be hoping, as the waters rise, still to be catching glimpses of themselves?

I had stood up and was manoeuvring Aunt Mavis towards the door. She was hard and bony. I thought — Aunt Mavis, if you want to be Ophelia, you will have to learn how to swim, not just to take your clothes off —

Then — This would be a good bit of advice for the Trotskyites?

When we were out in the hall, and the two women had followed us, Aunt Mavis began to try to sit on the stairs. I lowered her, straight-backed; and she stared out over her particular desert as if she were waiting for the annual fructification by the Nile.

I thought — But there are no seasons any more in that dining-room nor in Egypt —

One of the women said 'What do we do now?'

The other said 'I feel like a Chinese tart.'

Aunt Mavis was like one of those temples being covered by water: her outlines being eroded that were once cut into her brain —

One of the women said 'How's your father?'

I said 'He's all right.'

I thought — You were one of his snakes in the long grass?

She said 'You're very like him you know!'

I said 'Yes.'

I thought — Poor old mum.

The other woman said 'Can we get her upstairs?'

I said 'We can try.'

I thought — At least, you went sailing away on the high seas, my mother; and you were not tied to this lot out of pity —

Through the closed door we could hear the voices of what seemed to be Uncle Bill and the Editor and the MP talking to themselves, or to each other, in the dining-room, or on television.

I thought — Will you send me a message like a genie in a bottle, my mother? And that is where I will rest on the sea, when I am an albatross, or that dove?

XX

In the early hours of the morning I awoke in such despair that it was as if poison had been poured into my veins and I felt the best I could do was to open them and let the whole damned artificial lake out.

I was a cell, a sperm; that was being eaten by acid.

I thought — All these hopes, energies: a damp patch on the carpet.

There had been a boy at school who had tied himself to a railway line. He had put his neck on one rail and his ankles on the other and at the last minute he had tried to free himself but he could not untie his ankles and the train had run over them.

I thought — He was someone saying — For God's sake, look after me, by putting me out of my misery.

I tried to remember exactly what I had said at dinner. I had accused other people of being rotten. Whereas rottenness was now in myself. I was Aunt Mavis; waiting for someone to put their arms around me; having taken off her clothes and set fire to herself in a hotel lobby.

I thought — Of course we don't want to succeed: which is to have to adapt oneself to violent things like fire and water.

I found that I was longing for footsteps to come up the stairs: so I could throw my arms out; bury my head in any lap that would suck my blood like a vampire.

I thought — Despair is such aching for emptiness.

I had drunk too much whisky; then wine. The poison did not just happen in my veins; I had decided to pour it there.

I thought — Our unconscious is nuclear waste, leaking —

I could telephone to Dr Anders in the morning.

I could say — But I do not want to be made better! I want to become worse, to make an end of it!

I thought — Or is it the fact that I am coming out of some

protection that I cannot bear?

Every now and then it seemed that a guillotine was coming down at the back of my head. Then my head would fly off into a bucket. As if God had played some sort of golf shot.

And my head would lie in the hole grinning up at me.

— Hullo, hullo, do you hear me?

— Can you give me a hand up —

— I mean my give you a hand up —

— My slip: my Freudian slip —

If only I had not gone to Dr Anders; then I might have remained safe in my bathroom for ever.

I want to shout — Take it away! My head! That umbilicus at my windpipe!

But now, with my head in the bucket mouthing back at me —

— It is not just mind that is a complexity of matter —

— It is matter that is a simplicity of mind —

I thought I should try to go downstairs and make some cocoa. It was when I became immobile that there were these miseries.

I switched the light on. There was my room with its Dr Caligari ceilings.

I had half a dozen sleeping pills which I had pinched from my father or my mother. I thought — But if I want to go out fighting —

— How does one remember, if one endures this, it will be all right?

Some time during the night I got out my small store of pornographic literature. I thought — All right, you fuckers, you furies; if there is nothing so boring as you except King Agamemnon and Queen Clytemnestra —

— Then here is the story of Oedipus and the Belgian School-girls.

I wondered what it was they had done to Mr Perhaia.

Geese flew away over the Arctic: was it touch and go, they might spark off the world.

I thought — Well that's all right. I can now go down to the kitchen and make cocoa.

— What I must remember, from now on, is that I must live as

if my hands and feet were music —

— Or were supporting my own body like a sky or ceiling.

I had once seen an illustration of this, in a temple in Egypt.

But still, as Dante said — There are men's faces staring up through ice —

But I could get out of the kitchen window without being seen and go down towards the river.

In Bosch, in Breughel, there were devils eating people who were soft and compliant like fruit.

I thought — Oh come on, come on, my dark horse: you have my last straw: take me to my beloved!

I had got to the door. I thought — It is for identity's sake people fight: but millions die anyway on the carpet —

— Like seeds; like parachutes —

I was going down the stairs carrying my clothes and my slippers and my notebook. I thought — There is a rope, is there not, that goes up to the top part of the kitchen window?

— On it, I could climb out —

— Thus reversing these old images.

In the kitchen there was a light on.

I wondered if there were burglars come to steal something boring like state papers or old photographs —

There was in fact someone in the kitchen.

It was Mrs Washbourne.

I thought — She has come to cheer up Uncle Bill by acting out some old scandal —

— Or is she just someone who can't sleep; who has come to make some cocoa.

Mrs Washbourne, quite often, when there was work or anything to do, spent the night in the basement at Cowley Street.

She said 'I thought you were a burglar.'

I said 'I did too.'

She said 'I couldn't sleep.'

I said 'Nor could I.'

There was the long thin rope that went in a loop to the top of the high kitchen window. I thought — Perhaps I could make it seem as if I were about to hang myself.

Then — Ah, Mr Paragon, where have you gone with your Belgian Schoolgirls!

I said 'Actually, have some things been stolen, out of the house, recently?'

She said 'How did you hear that?'

I said 'What are they? Documents? Photographs?'

I had sat down at the kitchen table. Mrs Washbourne had turned back to the stove and seemed to be making cups of tea.

Then she suddenly sang, in an embarrassing contralto, ' — Tiger River, you have stolen my heart away — !'

I said 'I don't think it is Tiger River.'

She said 'What is it then?'

I said 'Dream River. Something River. I don't know.'

We sat on either side of the kitchen table. She gave me a cup of tea. I thought — When the bomb goes off, these must not be the sort of positions we will be remembered in —

I said 'Do you know a man called Jake Weatherby?'

She said 'Jake Weatherby!'

I thought — He's her lover? Her son? Having changed his name from something so unsuitable as Washbourne —

I said 'I think he's a reporter.'

She said 'He's not a reporter!'

I thought — Well he's not, is he, the man who put his arms round you at Mr Perhaia's party —

She said 'He used to know my husband.'

I said 'I didn't know you had a husband.'

She said 'Oh yes.'

I thought I might say — Where does he live? Libya?

She said 'Bert, your uncle's very tired.'

I said 'Yes.'

She said 'He'll kill himself if he goes on.'

I thought I might say — What, with that pistol?

I said 'Did you know my mother?'

She said 'Yes.'

I couldn't think what else to say.

Then she said 'Bert, you're not stammering.'

I said 'I know.'

She said 'Why not?'

I thought I might say — Because, if life were an umbilical cord, I have come to the end of my tether.

I said 'Perhaps Uncle Bill should have a rest. Jake Weatherby seemed to think he's in some danger.'

Mrs Washbourne put her head in her hands; she said 'Oh Bert I'm sorry! So sorry!'

I said 'What about?'

I thought — If only Mrs Washbourne could go out of the room, then I could do something sensible like climb out of the window and go down to the river.

She said 'He's had so much to put up with! He's been so cruelly maligned!'

I thought I might say — You can't say, cruelly maligned!

I said 'What are you going to do about Aunt Mavis?'

Mrs Washbourne looked up and said briskly 'Put her back in her cure, probably.'

She looked like someone who has been kicked.

I said 'Can you lend me a pound?'

She said 'What do you want a pound for?'

I said 'To have some money.'

I thought — If I take that rope, it might come in useful for carrying my pyjamas.

She said 'Oh Bert! It's so terrible we put on to you all this!'

Then she went out of the room. She seemed to be acting as if she were distressed.

I gave a tug on the rope at the window and the high-up part opened with a bang. A bit of glass half fell out, and hung there.

I thought — What, a guillotine?

If I could climb out through the main part of the window then I could put my arm back through the top part and close the latch of the main part: then I could pull the top part closed —

I thought — But what is the point of that bit that has broken?

— So that I can get in again?

— So, there are these coincidences!

But this was ridiculous.

I climbed out of the window.

I imagined — But isn't it reasonable after all that I would not want at this time of night to go out of the front door past that policeman?

I smoothed the broken bit of glass back into place: then I closed the main part of the window, and then the top part, gently.

I had taken the rope. I thought — Not to hang myself with, but to tie up a parcel.

I walked across the garden.

I thought — The point is, you go on some pilgrimage?

— For all those lost souls; for who have shot at whom, and how the bridesmaids have behaved —

I was wearing gym-shoes and was carrying my jeans and jersey.

I thought — I will change in the garden and I can wrap my pyjamas round my hands so as not to be cut by the glass on the top of the garden wall —

I remembered my father saying — What people are good at is getting keys from under doors and climbing down drain-pipes —

— Will we, one day, be good at getting keys from the wrong sides of doors that are in our minds?

I was going down towards the river. I had got over the garden wall quite easily.

I thought — Now I am truly one of the élite! I have no food, no home, no money —

I had just the pencil and notebook in which I sometimes wrote the things which came into my head —

— And launched them over the world on paper darts —

— Like doves or ravens from the ark, my father.

XXI

I wrote in my notebook a letter to Tammy Burns. I said —

Dear Tammy,

I have a project for the sort of film we talked about, which
might interest you.

Most films are boring now because a camera can't show
what a person is, what's inside him, how this might or might
not affect the outside world. Actors and film-makers try to
show what people do and what happens: but no one can talk
much about the mechanisms as it were between what people
are and what happens: the way someone perhaps by simply
being what he is can affect minds and hearts and not only of
people around him. And this is the most interesting thing in
the world, because without some feel of it people are like
furniture or animals; which they are not, because they do
things like making and looking at films.

My idea is that there should be at least two screens in the
first place perhaps side by side but then overlapping or one
moving inside the other so that for a time the other is like a
frame. And on one screen — the one that would later be in the
centre say — there would be a fairly ordinary story such as of a
man going off to war, as you might see in any old film; a
crusader or a cowboy perhaps trotting off in his awful armour;
he would be one of those men that actors like acting so much,
you know, all tragic and trussed up like a turkey. And on the
other screen — the one that would later be the frame perhaps
— there would be as it were the separate but quite closely
connected story of, say, the wife he has left behind; who as
soon as he has gone — on the other screen he would be
trundling across one of those tastefully orange deserts — the
wife would call in some frightful lover — this story would be

144

quite corny too you see; stories usually are; what's interesting is only what we make of them — a lover like one of those shaggy men you have to have more than a glimpse of to make sure it isn't a fig-leaf: and they, the wife and lover, would begin to make love; or to make those advances towards love that they'd feel they'd have to; what else can they do for ninety minutes? But really of course they might not want to at all; this is like life; to excuse ourselves, we make up morality. Well anyway, all this between the wife and the lover would be going on on one screen which would gradually begin to wrap round, or perhaps itself to be wrapped round by, the other screen: on which there would be the crusader or cowboy or whatever on his horse in his ghastly armour. But in what way by him, you see, if any, would the wife and lover be affected? Because they can, you see, go either this way or that: but perhaps not by their own willing. And the point of him, the crusader, would be that he too would be open: would be thinking — What am I doing this for? Why am I trundling across this desert in my armour? Why have I left my wife? Do I, or do I not, know she may have a lover? And he would both want and not want to die or to kill because of this; as if the desert were the arms of a lover. I mean he will not clearly think all this: but it would be going on somewhere inside him. And this, and not the trundle, is what would be interesting to an audience. And the wife would not quite know, too, but would feel — Here I am wrapped around the arms of my lover: what else am I doing this for except that there is inside me something dry and lost like my husband going off to war: that now knows where it is: because he is in a desert. But do I want this? What will make me choose? These things will not be seen clearly by the audience either; but they will be there, for the connections to be made if anyone wants to; and this will be possible, because the things will be shown side by side or one inside the other. And perhaps the audience will begin to feel, because they thus have the chance of making connections, what can be done about these things: within and about themselves even. For what else can choose? Well anyway; the crusader has arrived at his war. The wife is with her lover. But what have they to do with each other? If they do have

145

connections, this is the point, these will be such that have made him want either to live or to die; to make her want, or not, to go off with her lover. But these connections will be just the influence that the one might have had on the other throughout the whole of their lives: what they have ever been or become or made of themselves: the way in which the one might have grown within, or around (or not) the other; and so might influence him or her; because he or she is part of the other; even in a desert or in the arms of a lover. They would not really know this: they would know a bit what was, or was not, happening. I mean it is the whole life of the crusader, what he makes of himself, that will have become part of his wife and that will influence her: and it will be the whole of the life of the wife, what she has made of herself and in relation to her husband, that will be around him, in him, and that will make him want to live or kill or die. It will not be any direct action by the one that will affect the other: but just what the whole of them have been and are, their style and meaning. And perhaps this style is not so much of this or that: but just the fact that they know that they have a style and meaning. And they will demonstrate this by what they do on their own: but it will also, if it is inside them, be shown by the effect that it has on others.

Well there is the crusader at a town perhaps which he is laying siege to: he gets into some sort of position in which he can kill or not kill a victim: or if he does not kill, then perhaps the victim will kill him: and the wife on the outside or inside screen — or could the two screens writhe round each other so that they are like snakes that eat each other's tails or like lovers — by this time the wife perhaps is on the bed and is about to give in or not to her lover: part of her would have said yes but there would be also her husband inside her like a starved and violent child: would it not perhaps be better if he died? If she killed him? With her lover? But there he also is outside her with his sword raised about or not to kill his victim. And he will be thinking — no, not thinking; this is not the point; the point is what happens: what he has made of himself: all of this around and inside him: such as his wife — this will be what might stop him; or encourage him; give him reason to live or die — her arms around him or her lover; the child crying or dying inside her. Each of them everything they have ever been, and to each other. And then — this is the point — what was happening on one screen — or in the connections between the two — would become slightly bulging; bursting out from one screen to the other; like something living; like a cell; like something trying to emerge and create something different. Like a butterfly. The edge of the wife's nightdress, perhaps, would just flick out of her screen at the arm of the crusader who has his sword raised above his victim; might stir him on; might stop him. The crusader's raised elbow, perhaps, would just come out of his screen and nudge the wife on her bed; which would make her pause; if not to say just yes or no at least to think — no not think, it would have to be what happens — whether she would finally go away or not with her lover. Which would depend on what she and he, the husband, had ever been to each other; which would make her go or would stop her. The flick between the screens bulging outwards; like a propagation. And the crusader, within or around his wife, would or would not kill his victim. And the wife might get up and leave her lover; or might submit, with eyes looking out of the frame as if it were a window; either to help her husband or to wish him dead; she might want to free him or to be free of him; he might have wanted her to be unfaithful. This is not to do with morals, you see: it is to do with how people might see truly. The crusader might lay down his sword: might have killed, or been killed by, his victim. And his wife at the window would be looking out on a distant world. Having learned something perhaps about power; about victims. And her husband in the distant land living or dying perhaps but being peaceful. They having just nudged one another. By what they had ever been. And they would both know this, and not know it. But what does the audience know. Some perhaps might be able to know it: by what they have ever been.

I would have to work out more of the details; and of the story. But what makes stories boring is the way things happen one after the other without any freedom; there's no chance of anything being different. Whereas in life what's interesting is how so many things happen all at once; and it's by this, and by what you are, that you choose; you can't choose this or that to happen perhaps, but you can choose what you are to be interested in. And so make lively. This, if not action, is always possible. And perhaps it's a caring or not for everything that is the choice: not for this or that or for only loved ones; but caring or not for everything because caring is just caring and the only other choice is not.

Now there's something I've just thought of here that may not work. What if the audience were told that they themselves could affect the outcome; were told that by pressing a lever or button or something by their seats they might make happen or not happen (I was going to write happy!) what they wanted to make happen (or happy!) on the screens — would the crusader live or die; would the wife or not go off with her lover. And the levers or buttons would be connected to nothing of course; except to a machine that would record the members of the audience's decisions. But this would be the point: it would be like life. People would know of course that everyone else would be pulling levers; so that they should not be surprised when things did not turn out as they liked. But still, what they had chosen would be recorded: and it would be this — this is the point: this is what their influence is! — that might affect them; in their own bodies, their minds. The film of course would be just whatever the film-maker had made of it; like God; but people would still be making what they wanted of themselves; by their decisions; and this would be possible, because they would know their decisions which had been recorded. They would know — You get what you want, you see: in yourselves, look — you are this or that sort of person! You want these other people to live or die! You want yourselves to be lively or deathly. This would be the nudge, you see, recorded: both in, and affecting, their minds: and also the outside world —

For what if one had a big enough computer in fact so that the audience did affect possible outcomes on the screen; or in the world, according to averages; is this like life? With everyone pulling their own levers; and so seeming to balance out into entropy. But still, there is liveliness. And this would be in the minds of people who, by what they have ever been, by what they have made of themselves, do feel free; and so see that they stand back from entropy; and by giving it a nudge, might tip the scales down one side or the other. But this would require some learning.

Well, it's five o'clock in the morning and I'm sitting in Embankment Gardens and I'm cold and my pencil has run out and I'm having to sharpen it with my fingernails.

I enjoyed our meeting the other day.

Love

Bert

P.S. Do you know the story of Plato's cave? Well, why didn't the people in the cave think of something like using their fingers to make shadows on the wall? Then might not what was going on outside in the sun have come into the cave to see what was funny?

I thought of a few more PS's but my pencil was so blunt it was behaving like an india rubber.

I needed a stamp and an envelope.

I thought — Perhaps I will be able to swap my rope and pyjamas for a stamp and an envelope at some stationers.

It was really later than five o'clock in the morning. It had been five o'clock when I had started.

Soon, I could ring up Dr Anders.

I walked up and down by the river.

I thought — What have I given birth to? Some baby that, like my screen, has two heads?

— Will it come up like the sun, or like the face of a drunk man from behind a table —

Dr Anders had left me her telephone number. When the time came to telephone her, I had to reverse the charges because I had no money. I found out from the operator that the number was in Cambridge.

'Dr Anders?'

'Yes.'

'This is — '

'Hallo.'

I did not quite know if I was stammering. I seemed to be listening.

'I'm sorry to telephone you so early.'

'That's all right.'

'And I'm sorry I've had to reverse the charges.'

'Why?'

'I haven't any money.'

'Then why are you sorry?'

I thought — Here we go again! Good heavens!

I said 'I felt terrible last night. But now I'm better. But I thought I'd ring you anyway.'

She said 'What sort of terrible?'

'Well, suicidal.'

'What did you feel?'

'As if I wanted to cut my head off. With a guillotine. To stop myself thinking or feeling.'

Dr Anders said nothing.

I said 'And then it all got tied up, as usual, with sex.'

She said 'But now it's better.'

I said 'Yes.'

She said 'What did you do last night?'

I said 'I had dinner with Uncle Bill and Aunt Mavis.'

She said nothing.

I thought — All right! But I've got out! Haven't I?

I said 'Then I went down on to the embankment and wrote something I'm quite pleased with.'

She said 'Good.'

I thought — Well, is that all? Is a birth so simple?

She said 'I'll be back on Friday.'

I said 'I thought it was Monday.'

She said 'No, it's earlier.'

I thought — Well, that's even better.

Then — My two-headed baby will be all right?

She said 'Have you got anything to do tonight?'

I said 'Yes as a matter of fact, there's the Annual General Meeting of the Young Trotskyites.'

She said 'Will you go to the Annual General Meeting of the Young Trotskyites?'

I said 'Yes.'

She said 'It sounds like the title of a song.'

I thought — What an extraordinary thing for Dr Anders to say!

She said 'Oh yes, and ask your Uncle Bill for money.'

I said 'Why is the Annual General Meeting of the Young Trotskyites like the title of a song?'

She said 'It reminds me of when I was young.'

Then — 'Tell me about your baby, what you have written, on Friday.'

XXII

The Annual General Meeting of the Young Trotskyites was held in a dance hall which had been specially arranged for the occasion: a long table had been put on the stage where bands usually played, and rows of seats had been spread over the dance floor. There were families in neat and quiet rows as if they had once, years ago, heard rumours of a divine visitation but now what they more appreciated was the outing.

Above the table on the stage was an enormous banner announcing that Trotsky had been killed in 1940.

I was still taking care for some reason or other that people should not recognise me: so I had waited in the streets till I thought the meeting had started — these meetings always started late because like this the audience might be encouraged to imagine a divine visitation — and then I hurried in and sat on a chair on an outside aisle behind a pillar. I thought — Do I imagine myself as an angel, waiting in a courtyard?

Of course, the meeting had not started.

On the platform was Brian Alick; and, briefly, Sally Rogers.

I thought — But did not Sally suggest that she was no longer a friend of the Trotskyites? This would not, of course, mean she was no longer a friend of the Trotskyites; but why had she bothered to suggest it?

One of the odd things about Trotskyites was that although they claimed to be a revolutionary movement they were always going on about what had happened in 1940. I wondered — But might not this, to them, be as important as the question of whether or not the Holy Ghost had two fathers?

There were all these quiet, composed people like clones waiting to be sent out into the world and take it over. I thought — But they should be ideas, not people?

Sally Rogers had been talking with Brian Alick. They had

seemed like conspirators plotting against the bare back wall of a stage.

I thought — But they should be watching the audience as if it were their unconscious to see whether or not the time had come for their ideas to go out into the world —

The meeting had not yet started; apparently because there was some slight disturbance at the door.

That morning, afternoon, I had gone to a public library. I had managed to get from the librarian some clean paper and an envelope. I had copied out my letter to Tammy Burns.

I had wondered — Am I using words in a way that will give birth to things in the mind whether or not there is the sort of cinema screen I am writing about?

The librarian had also given me a new pencil; but would not accept my pyjamas and rope in exchange. So I had thought — It would not be proper to ask her for a stamp.

Then — How, in my film, would I get someone to give me a stamp?

— Once, I would have stammered?

But I did not want to stammer.

I had carried my bulging envelope through streets and had thought — Now, in this strange city, what other escaped prisoners will recognise and make friends with me —

Brian Alick came forward on the platform. He said 'Comrades — '

I thought — But if he is Sheila's lover, could I not, in my film, hoist him with a corner of my smile coming out from my screen; and leave him slightly above his platform like St Theresa?

'Comrades, we have been informed by our friends here the police — '

He paused as if to let the audience make sure he was being funny —

' — that they have had a message that a bomb has been placed in the auditorium. Now I myself give this story absolutely no credence whatsoever — '

Another pause: so that the audience might know he was being serious —

' — nor, I am glad to say, do the police.'

I thought — So the audience, blown to and fro, thinks nothing, feels nothing; admires the technique.

'I regard it as just one more attempt at disruption on the part of I shall not say our enemies but I shall not also say our friends in the Revolutionary Movement — '

Brian Alick frowned, severely.

I thought — The point is that no one is exactly sure what he wants to say; so they are open to just the technique.

'However, I believe I should give this warning so that anyone who wishes can leave the auditorium.'

Brian Alick gazed round.

— Is it you? Is it you? —

Then he sat down behind the table.

I thought — What is it that is actually happening then?

People were unmoved and unmoving in the audience: I thought — Do they believe, if they are elect, what is it if they die?

After a time Brian Alick stood up again.

'Then shall we get on with the meeting?'

For some time the faint disturbance at the door had been increasing. I thought it was to do with the police and the bomb.

'Comrades, we are gathered together for this our anniversary — '

Once I had been with Sheila to a street meeting of the Young Trotskyites when they had been attacked by the Patriotic Front. There had been a fight in which people seemed to be reaching for each other's faces as if to snatch trophies there. One man had wrapped his coat around him and had run into the restraining arms of police as if he was bouncing on a trampoline.

' — to reaffirm the programme of this our revolutionary movement — '

There were one or two people moving up the aisles like security men. Voices had been raised by the door.

I thought — But if the proper environment for all this is the mind —

The people each side of Brian Alick on the platform were watchful as if they had machine-guns.

— It is you — It is you —

' — but first, you will bear with me if I deal with some business still in our midst.'

I thought — This is all some allegory; of something for which we have no language.

Brian Alick began to refer to people who might or might not have betrayed Trotsky in 1940.

I thought — Politicians, like theologians, have as yet no way of talking directly about things that are in their hearts and minds.

Brian Alick's speech continued. Sometimes he shouted: sometimes his voice sank low. I found it difficult to hear his words. I thought — He is spraying us with bullets: like romantic music —

Then — It is something like music we can take back to make us lively in our minds —

Then, turning in my mind away from Brian Alick's speech and thinking — But if I stay here will I be like one of those bodies curled up when the lava comes down: is it enough just to turn like Tammy Burns with my profile to the music —

— So that when the machine-guns open up from the people on the platform —

— How many want to save themselves? Or from a bomb? —

— To take hold of the levers of their hearts and minds and climb up on them as if notes of music were a ladder —

— So that when the bullets come over from the people with machine-guns —

— Duck —

— Bullets bounce off water —

— Then look for a hand in the rubble —

— Is it you: is it you —

— A hand, where you thought was a trinket —

— As in Shakespeare's recognition plays when the hand comes alive and takes your own —

— after the wind has blown the rest of the leaves into the trenches they have dug for themselves —

— Hullo, hullo, I wondered if you remembered me —

— Oh yes, I've never loved anyone else you see —

155

There was still this disturbance at the door. Then I turned and saw Judith Ponsonby.

She was in a seat off the aisle about three or four rows behind me. She was smiling and nodding at me; as if she had been trying to make me turn round for some time.

I looked back at the platform.

I thought — What happens when you win? When the ball slots into the right hole —

— when the arrow flies by itself to the centre of the target; when you have not been thinking; when you have been your own music —

I turned back and smiled at Judith Ponsonby.

— with her bright child's face: that with a broken wing would lead others to the precipice for the sake of her children —

Brian Alick had begun to shout like a man either in, or for, a strait-jacket.

— between the pillars of the dance hall that sort of shaft coming down: a dove with an olive branch pointing to a land-fall —

— a girl with arrows and the bow-string against her breast —

The disturbance at the door seemed to be being caused by a man with a red beard trying to get in. He was now coming down the aisle towards us.

I realised — He is one of those shaggy men like cinema technicians who were at Sally Rogers' party.

— Changing from one screen to another —

— Laying hold of her —

— But now, I will not lose her.

The man with the red beard had taken hold of Judith Ponsonby and was trying to pull her from her seat.

I stood up.

One of the security men came up and took hold of the man with the red beard.

Judith Ponsonby, between them, seemed to shrug her shoulders at me.

I thought — She is like the girl in *Petrouchka*.

Brian Alick paused for a moment in his speech: then went on shouting.

I followed Judith Ponsonby and the man with a red beard and the security guard up the aisle and towards the door.

Then — But where do we go now? She has been blown like a sycamore seed; we are whizzing up the cliff with the wind taking us —

By the exit door, halfway into the street, there was an argument again between the various men round Judith Ponsonby. The security man had been joined by a policeman. Judith Ponsonby turned from the bearded man's arm as if she were Jonah half out of the whale.

'Hullo — '

'Hullo — '

'I wondered if you remembered me.'

She said 'Oh yes, I was looking for you you see!'

'You were?'

'Yes.'

I said 'Can you have supper?'

I thought — To pay for it, I can murder some old woman like a pawnbroker.

She said 'Oh I'd love to, but I seem to be sort of tied up as you see!'

I said 'Shall I rescue you?'

She said 'Oh will you please!'

She looked despairing.

I thought — But have I not known she would have to hurt me.

Then she said 'But not just yet.'

I said 'I'll ring you.'

She said 'Will you promise?'

Then she picked the man's hand carefully off her arm as if it were a burr. She began looking in her pockets.

I thought — She controls things like those people with telephone wires underground —

Then I said 'Can you by any chance lend me some money to buy a stamp?'

She said 'If you promise to give it back.'

She pulled from her pocket a five-pound note. She held it out to me.

I said 'That's too much.'

She said 'The last seven numbers on it are my telephone number.'

I said 'How extraordinary!'

She said 'Yes isn't it.'

I said 'What are the odds against that?'

She said 'Millions, I suppose.'

I said 'Yes, they would be.'

I took the note, carefully.

She said 'But I might have gone to live at the place, you know, specially where there is this number.

I said 'Like those men who buy cars.'

She said 'Exactly.' Then — 'But that would have been almost as difficult.'

I said 'But now I won't be able to use it to get a stamp.'

She said 'No you won't, will you.'

The man with the red beard and the security guard and the policeman were watching us.

She said 'You might be able to raise a loan on it.'

I said 'I will.'

She said 'You won't forget to ring me?'

I said 'No.'

The man with the red beard began pulling her.

She said 'What do you carry that rope for?'

I said 'To rescue people with.'

She said 'I'll remember that.'

XXIII

When I got back to Cowley Street it was late in the evening. I had been walking through streets with kings and queens coming together in my head. I thought I could say to Dr Anders — It is this that is music: when you are dancing on notes as if they are footholds on a mountain.

Judith Ponsonby had half held her hand out for my rope; with the man with the red beard tugging her.

In one of the streets near Cowley Street there was a huge car parked. I imagined it was like Tammy Burns'; but I thought this was overdoing it.

Outside Uncle Bill's house was a small crowd as there sometimes was at times of crisis (I thought — There is a crisis I haven't noticed?) so I decided to go round to the back and climb over the garden wall where I had got out that morning. Then I could put my hand through the cracked piece of glass in the kitchen and open the window from inside.

I thought — Thus accidents work out to be useful: like the giraffes that have long necks when there are leaves only on the top of trees —

— But this too depends on security arrangements being inadequate?

From the street the garden wall was seven or eight feet high. I still had my pyjamas with me. I could put these on the glass on the top of the wall again and take a running jump and be like a man flying off with a ball and chain through the universe.

There was a light on in Aunt Mavis' room. The rest of the house seemed to be in darkness.

I thought I might stand in the garden beneath Aunt Mavis' window and say — I am Romeo come from the dead —

I was still in the garden when Aunt Mavis did in fact appear at the window. She pulled up the bottom sash and looked out.

She appeared to have no clothes on.

I thought — She is like some sign of the Zodiac?

I wondered, if I stayed still, whether she might fade away like other impressions of magic.

After a time Aunt Mavis moved back into her room and closed the window.

I walked across the garden.

I thought — There is some image in my mind about this: the back of a house where windows light up for a moment and things are seen as if in memory and then disappear —

The light in Aunt Mavis' room went out. A second or two later the light came on on the second-floor landing. Aunt Mavis was going down the stairs. She still had no clothes on. She had put on a large flowered hat.

I thought — She will go out into the street, where there is that small crowd waiting.

— And thus expose the pretences of this corrupt society —

— But should I not get in through the kitchen window quickly?

The light went off on the stairs: the light came on in the first-floor drawing room.

I thought — What is this image like death cut off at the waist and wearing a hat; rolling down a slope to some black hole at the bottom —

I was trying to get the piece of glass out from the kitchen window. It was held, delicately, by dry putty.

— There are burglar alarms that still do not go off?

When I was in the house I went through into the hall. There were no lights anywhere.

I thought — These were just images playing tricks in my unconscious?

It was about ten-thirty at night. There might be some secretaries watching television in the basement.

I thought I should whisper, as though I were anxious about a ghost — Aunt Mavis?

In the hall there was a faint light from the street outside. The door was open into Uncle Bill's study.

I thought that if I turned the lights on, and Aunt Mavis was there, she might be seen from the street outside or make a dash for it.

Also — If you wake sleepwalkers, do not their walls collapse like paper?

I said 'Aunt Mavis?'

'Oh you did frighten me!'

She said this quite calmly. She was behind the door into the study; where she seemed to have been waiting.

She said 'Were you all right darling? Were you cold?'

I did not understand this. I thought she must be projecting on to me the fact that she had no clothes on.

She said 'Did they treat you all right?'

She came towards me in the hall. I thought I should stay between her and the front door.

She said 'Did they give you food or anything?'

She seemed to be pulling gloves on. Her skin hung on her like furs. I wondered for a moment — She really does have no clothes on?

I said 'Don't go out.'

She said 'I've got proof.'

I said 'Of what?'

She said 'Darling, you were only the first!'

I found that I did not like the idea of touching her. I tried to rationalise this — She might scream?

She had stopped in front of a mirror as if to arrange her hat.

I said 'The first what?'

She said 'She gives him money.'

I said 'Who gives him money?'

She said 'Her husband's very rich.'

When she moved towards the door I put out a hand and took hold of her.

I thought — Not too bad: like oysters.

I said 'It's cold outside.'

She said 'You won't be able to stop me.'

I said 'Aunt Mavis, you're drunk.'

She said 'What do you mean I'm drunk?'

I said 'Aunt Mavis, you haven't got any clothes on.'

She turned to one side and sat in a chair by the front door. I let go of her. She held her head in profile. There was a noise of what seemed to be laughter from beyond the front door.

She said 'No one's ever said that to me.'

I said 'Why shouldn't you be drunk? As a matter of fact, I don't see why you shouldn't have no clothes on.'

She said 'As a matter of fact I'm parched.'

I said 'Well why don't you have another drink then?'

When she turned her head towards me I had the impression (it was quite dark) that her eyes were bleeding.

She said 'I wanted to dance and sing.'

I said 'Well dance and sing then.'

I felt suddenly as if what I was doing was putting my head down on her shoulder and laughing as the man had done to me at Mr Perhaia's party.

I said 'What was it you wanted to dance and sing?'

Then it seemed that there was something quite different going on: some excavation by men with pick-axes, clicking.

I wondered — Is this what Dr Anders hears?

She said 'Oh God, you don't want to see it, do you?'

I said 'Yes, what's it like?'

She said 'It's awful!'

She stood up. She raised one arm above her head.

Then she put her head on her chest and made a noise like someone retching.

I said 'That's not right is it?'

She straightened and raised her arm again. Then she lowered it.

I thought — She is acting?

Then — Get it out: Get it out —

She said 'They can do what they like to me!'

I said 'Is that the title of a song?'

Then she seemed to topple, onto her hands and knees on the floor.

In this position she was like a wooden horse with nails through its eyes.

What I had been doing all this time with Aunt Mavis had been so much in the dark — the darkness of the hall, the darkness of my mind, the darkness of some way that I thought might be opened through which I could help her — that I had hardly noticed that there were now stronger noises from the street outside.

I had gone to the bottom of the stairs and I held out a hand to Aunt Mavis.

I said 'Come on up to bed.'

She arched her back and seemed to try to be sick.

I thought — Or she is like a fish with a line down to her stomach —

I said 'You've got it out now.'

She said 'Why, what did they put in it?'

I thought — A worm? An asp?

I said 'That sounds like another song.'

I went to a hatstand where there were some coats and I took one down and held it out to her.

She straightened, still on her knees. She said 'You don't mind?'

A key was turning in the lock of the front door.

I had been so intent on not breaking the fragile connection I had with Aunt Mavis that I did not care about anyone's coming in, except that they should not hurt Aunt Mavis —

I had thought — Pull at the line too violently and you'll kill her —

Then the front door opened and Brian Alick came in.

At least it seemed to be Brian Alick. It also seemed I must be having an hallucination.

A light was switched on. Aunt Mavis, wearing just her hat, was on her knees facing the front door.

Some flashlights went off.

Brian Alick, by Aunt Mavis, was staring at her. Then he looked at me.

I thought — This is precisely what is happening?

Then Sheila came in.

I was sure it was Sheila. I could tell by the way she stood with her toes turned in.

I thought — But where is this happening?

More flashlights seemed to go off outside.

Brian Alick turned to the front door.

163

Sheila was looking at me as if she did not recognise me.

Brian Alick tried to push the door closed. It seemed to bump up against someone else coming in.

Uncle Bill came in. He was holding his nose.

I thought — We are in someone else's time-warp?

More and more people seemed to be trying to push in.

I thought — A film has broken down: there are too many people in my maze, or in a telephone box —

Uncle Bill and Brian Alick and Sheila were in a group by the front door. They were looking at Aunt Mavis.

Mrs Washbourne was calling 'Let me in!' She had got an arm through the door.

I went and put the coat I was holding around Aunt Mavis.

Mrs Washbourne appeared, struggling.

Uncle Bill said 'And keep that door shut!'

Sheila said 'There's no need to push!'

Mrs Washbourne was saying 'What are you doing here?'

I realised she was talking to me.

Brian Alick said 'Let's get out.'

Uncle Bill said 'No.'

I don't know how long all this took. I suppose only a few seconds. Time stretches: then people are at home again in their environment.

Uncle Bill said 'Take her upstairs.'

I said 'I was going to.'

I thought — Till you all came in with your pick-axes and gumboots.

Brian Alick said 'All right.'

Sheila said 'What are you doing here?'

I realised, after a time, that she too was talking to me.

Mrs Washbourne said 'Bert, we thought you'd been kidnapped.'

Uncle Bill said 'We better have a post-mortem; though no one's actually dead yet, are they?'

XXIV

Uncle Bill said 'But did, or didn't, anyone see if they got a photograph.'

Brian Alick said 'I didn't.'

Sheila said 'I saw a flash.'

Mrs Washbourne said 'Flash is the word.'

Uncle Bill said 'Nellie!'

We were in the drawing room on the first floor. Mrs Washbourne was standing by the window and was holding one side of the curtain back as if she were a secret-service agent in a film. Sheila and Brian Alick were sitting straight-backed on the sofa.

'There was definitely a photographer.'

'Who was he, do you know?'

'Not that unattractive photographer.'

'Nellie!'

'Can you find out?'

'How?'

'You've got contacts, haven't you?'

Uncle Bill was by the fireplace holding a glass of whisky. He had handed round whisky to the others. Every now and then he moved as if he had forgotten his whisky, and drops like a blessing flew out over the carpet.

'Who was supposed to be with Mavis this evening?'

'No one.'

'Why not?'

'Why should they be?'

'I must make it clear we have absolutely no interest in any of this.'

'We came here to find out about Bert.'

'What was it about Bert; Nellie?'

I was sitting in a straight-backed chair opposite the fire. I thought — I will be here like a secretary just to take things down: or like that figure on the banks of the Nile to tell the world what are true and what are untrue messages —

'I asked our two friends here — '

'Sheila — '

'Brian Alick — '

'To come round?'

'Does this matter now?'

'Of course.'

'Why?'

'I don't know if this aspect worries you — '

'What about Mavis — '

'We understood he hadn't been seen — '

'What about?'

' — for two days. We came round here — '

Aunt Mavis had been taken up to her room. A doctor had been sent for. One of the secretaries had stayed with her: then the rest of us had gathered in the drawing room as if in the last act of a play about murderers and detectives.

'What do you mean he hadn't been seen for two days?'

'He was here last night. He disappeared.'

'People don't just disappear.'

'He was having dinner.'

'He went out of the front door — '

'I thought you said a window.'

'I said he couldn't have got out of the window.'

'Why don't you ask him then?'

'Are we here to talk about Bert?'

'That's exactly what we were supposed to be here for.'

'Did anyone, or not, see whether they got a photograph?'

I thought — Are Cabinet meetings like this? People say what they want, and seem to listen; then gas or music comes in through little pipes in the ceiling —

'What happened last night?'

'I don't know how much anyone could see through that door.'

'He was in the kitchen.'

'How far does a flash reach?'

'I thought you said he was at dinner.'

'Then when he went out of the front door — '

166

'Not out of the window — '

'You could certainly see in through that door.'

'Why?'

'What do you mean why?'

'Look we're not here to talk about Bert.'

'But we are.'

'But things have happened since then.'

'I thought you said he was in the house all the time.'

'I said it looked like it.'

'There was this screech of tyres, and the noise of a car driving away.'

'A screech and a car — '

'If he hadn't got out of the window, it looked as if he was in the house — '

'But he wasn't.'

'There was a man at the door.'

'I thought you said it was a car.'

'I think we're talking about different things.'

'It wasn't us who wanted to come here you know.'

I thought — Is it the point of a committee that it should just go on? Is that why you don't ask me?

Sheila said 'Can't you stop the printing of a photograph?'

Brian Alick said 'What, in this democratic society?'

Mrs Washbourne said 'I'm glad you think so.'

Uncle Bill said 'How did you three know each other?'

Mrs Washbourne left the window and came and sat down on the other side of the fire opposite Sheila and Brian Alick.

I thought — It was she who got the information about my friendship with the Trotskyites?

Then Uncle Bill said 'Where were you Bert?'

I said 'When?'

He said 'Today.'

I said 'I was at the Annual General Meeting of the Young Trotskyites.'

Brian Alick said 'He couldn't have been.'

Uncle Bill said 'Why not?'

Brian Alick said 'Well, what happened at the AGM?'

Sheila said 'We thought you'd been kidnapped.'

Brian Alick said 'We didn't!'

Mrs Washbourne said 'What did you think then?'

Sheila said 'We heard a shot: then a car drive away.'

Uncle Bill said 'At the AGM?'

I said 'There was a bomb scare: but nothing happened.'

Brian Alick said 'That's right.'

Mrs Washbourne said 'But that was when he was having dinner here.'

I said 'No, that was the evening before.'

Uncle Bill said 'A shot? A bomb scare?'

Sheila said 'He was definitely being followed.'

Brian Alick said 'Not by us.'

Mrs Washbourne said 'I was afraid he might do some injury to himself.'

I opened my mouth to say — But I was not being followed! Then it seemed as if I would not stammer, and then that this was not worth saying.

Uncle Bill went to the window and raised a corner of the curtain as if he were a secret-service man looking out.

Brian Alick said 'Do they know who we are?'

Mrs Washbourne said 'I rang up Sally Rogers.'

Uncle Bill said 'Who?'

Sheila said 'You know Sally Rogers — '

Uncle Bill said 'Does she now!'

I began laughing.

I thought — We are tickled by glands? By tiny angels pushing pumps like men in pubs?

Uncle Bill said 'Now let's get this straight. You made contact with our friends here because you thought you had reason to be anxious about Bert. He'd disappeared: out of a kitchen: out of a door: there was a car —. So you two came round here — '

I said 'I was all right.'

Mrs Washbourne said 'I'm sure you were Bert.'

Uncle Bill said 'Anyone want some more?'

'Yes please.'

'Yes please.'

Uncle Bill handed round the whisky.

He said 'The point is what do we do now.'

After a time Brian Alick said 'What I don't understand is, if you thought he was in the house all the time, why you telephoned.'

Mrs Washbourne said 'But the point is he wasn't.'

Sheila said 'That was the mystery!'

Uncle Bill said 'How did you put up with your ordeal, Bert, did these fellows give you the electrical treatment, what?'

Brian Alick said 'I don't know what effect all this will have on you, but it will certainly embarrass us.'

Mrs Washbourne said 'When did you last see him?'

I said 'Why do anything?'

I thought — Is this like upsetting the chess-table? All the lights in the auditorium coming on?

Uncle Bill said 'Why do anything about what.'

I said 'The photograph. Of Aunt Mavis.'

They all seemed to think.

Then Brian Alick said 'You mean, what can we do about the photograph anyway — '

I said 'No, I mean no one will believe it anyway.'

They all seemed to think.

I wondered — Is this what my sister meant when she said I would become insufferable?

Sheila said 'Surely you can find out.'

Mrs Washbourne said 'How?'

I said 'People only believe what they want to believe. Or what it's in their interests to believe. Whose interests will it be in, for God's sake, to believe a photograph like that?'

I thought — Someone magical?

Then — They will think about this for a time: then talk about something different.

I said 'The whole thing will seem to be a joke: and so in some quite different category.'

Uncle Bill said 'You mean do nothing?'

Brian Alick said 'And it'll fly away?'

I thought — Ah, you think you're mocking me!

I said 'It'll be like one of those photographs you stick your head through on a pier.'

After a time Mrs Washbourne said 'Bert!'

Uncle Bill walked round the room with his head down, smiling.

169

Brian Alick said 'It's true, of course, that one can fake a photograph.'

Sheila said 'Indeed.'

Brian Alick said 'Sheila!'

I said 'The point is that people aren't interested in what's true — '

I thought — Oh keep quiet, this is not a moral, but a theological problem.

Uncle Bill sat down beside Sheila and Brian Alick. He pulled out his pipe.

I said 'I mean people have known for years, haven't they, about Aunt Mavis doing things like getting drunk and taking her clothes off? But who on earth has wanted to talk about it?'

Uncle Bill said 'Yes that's true.'

After a time Mrs Washbourne said 'Bert, how did you get back into the house then?'

I said 'When I got out of the kitchen window there was a bit of glass that cracked, so I could put my hand back in through it and get at the latch.'

Uncle Bill said 'But why did you want to?'

I said 'Because at the door there was a policeman.'

Uncle Bill seemed to think about this.

Brian Alick said 'There isn't a policeman at the back?'

Uncle Bill said 'Well, it was extremely good of you two to come along!'

Sheila said 'Oh it's been very nice to see the place really!'

Mrs Washbourne said 'How many other photographs has anyone got by the way?' But no one seemed to want to pay attention to this.

Brian Alick said 'Well thanks for the whisky.'

Uncle Bill did his trick of suddenly taking his pipe out of his mouth and looking as if he had broken a tooth and swallowed by mistake some poison hidden in it.

I thought — What is magical is when what one is talking about at the same time seems to happen; and we are so unused to this, that it is like seeing ourselves looking down at ourselves in the maze —

Then — But with all this magic, will Aunt Mavis now be able to change: or will Uncle Bill just be all right?

170

XXV

I thought — Now carry me, my dark horse, to my beloved!

Dr Anders said — 'Were it not for your imagery about birds, I would say that you looked like the cat that has swallowed the canary.'

I had walked all the way to Dr Anders' house and it was as if I were slightly above myself like one of those bird-songs which lead heroes through forests.

I had begun to tell Dr Anders something of what had happened; and then had stopped; as if the theatre had packed up and gone home through lack of interest.

I said 'But I must get out.'

She said 'Where do you want to get to?'

I said 'Some university. I don't know.'

She said 'Which?'

I said 'Any.'

I thought — And it is because of lack of interest that there are in my mind no more dull stories about pistols going off and papers being stolen and flashlight photographs being taken: or a son's tearing his eyes out behind closed doors, o my mother.

Dr Anders said 'And what would you read there?'

I said 'I don't know.'

I thought — But now, don't I?

I said 'I don't think I want to do philosophy. I think reason is good at saying what things are not, but not really at saying what things are.'

I thought — Do words have to wrap round each other like making love; like poetry?

Then — But I can do this?

Dr Anders said nothing.

I said 'I think I'd like to do biology or chemistry or physics.'

I thought — Dr Anders' silences are when she is pleased?

She might have been listening to music?

I said 'There was this idea, you know, that I should wait a year before going to university so that I could come to you; to be straightened out; to be cured. Well, of course, I'm not cured; but I don't think my stammer will really worry me very much any more, do you?'

I thought — It can accept, can't it, poor thing, that words might press together like making love, like poetry?

I said 'The trouble is, if I went to university, I might not be able to go on coming to you.'

I thought — Do I believe this?

Also — I'm not doing this just to be nice to her, am I?

I felt suddenly as if I might cry.

She said 'Have you heard the results of your exams yet?'

I said 'Yes.'

'And what are they?'

'Good.'

I thought — Once I could not have said just — Good!

It was as if she were sitting on some egg waiting for it to be hatched.

She said 'So you could go to a university now?'

'Presumably.'

I thought — But she has understood this, hasn't she, that if I go to a university now, it will be almost impossible for me to go on seeing her?

— And that however helped I am, if one is taken apart and put together again it takes time, doesn't it, to get used to this, o my father —

I said 'But I haven't put in any of the applications yet and I suppose it's too late now.'

She said 'Surely your uncle or Mrs Washbourne could pull strings for you?'

I said 'I don't want them to pull strings.'

She seemed, on top of her egg, to be unaccountably embarrassed.

I thought — Not because I might cry?

She said 'You know this week I've been in Cambridge — '

Then I thought — I'm not going to be able to bear this —

172

I said 'Yes.'

She said 'Well, I did have the opportunity as a matter of fact to make one or two enquiries for you.'

I thought — Did I know this all the time?

Then — It is happiness that is not bearable?

I said 'Yes.'

She said 'And they seemed to think, the people whom I talked to, that there would not be much difficulty in your getting in to some university now; someone with your qualifications.'

I thought — If it is happiness, I will bear it?

But also — Will I go on seeing you?

She said 'You would have to go and convince them of course; show them your results. But I've no doubt you'll be able to do this.'

I thought suddenly — This person to whom you spoke: is it the person through whom my sister put me in touch with you; her lover?

I said 'At Cambridge?'

She said 'Yes. Or anywhere.'

I said 'But doesn't the term start in a week or so?'

I thought — Ah well, wait: you still don't know all the outside world can do for you —

She said 'It would be difficult for you, of course, to come up here each day.'

I thought — But to hope was not unreasonable?

She seemed to be doing the breathing exercises which I sometimes did for my stammer: in, one two: hold it, three four: out, five six seven eight —

I said 'I thought analysis was supposed to go on for about three years.'

She said 'Ah, this isn't an old-fashioned analysis — '

I wanted to ask — What is it then?

She said 'You want to go on seeing me?'

I thought for a moment I would not answer this: can one say — I am lonely?

I said 'Yes.'

Then I said 'But I'll survive.'

Her eyes were closed. I thought — She is about to give birth: which is what happens to those figures on the banks of the Nile, when the waters break —

She said 'I expect you'll go on stammering for a while. Perhaps, in a way, always. When it suits you. I mean, it's one of your ways of dealing with the outside world; and not always a bad one. But I don't think you'll stammer much any more when it's important for you not to; and I don't think it'll worry you very much even when you do. You'll make the best of it.'

I thought I might say — Granted.

Then I thought — Is her egg, now, when it is about to hatch, going to be one of those things that one cannot say?

She said 'You know, when you first came to me, and I said I'd given up private patients?'

I said 'Yes.'

She said 'Well I had.'

I thought — Oh my bird, my dark horse, don't lose me in this forest!

We were silent for a time.

I said 'So why did you take me on?'

Then — 'No: why were you giving up private patients?'

She said 'Because I'd been offered a job at a university.'

I tried to say — I see.

I thought — Animals! Dragons! listen to my music!

She said 'A teaching job.'

I said 'I'm not going to be able to bear this.'

She said 'Oh yes you are.'

I thought — All the lights have gone out in my theatre. We have already gone home.

She said 'It seemed reasonable for me to say that I would take you on for these few months, and then we would see.'

I thought — And then we did.

I wanted to ask again — What made you take me?

I said 'So you will be at this university if I go too. I can go on seeing you?'

After a time she said 'Yes.'

I said 'Is the person you spoke to in Cambridge the same as the friend of my sister's?'

174

She said ' "The same" sounds magical.'

I said 'Well, is it?'

Then I said 'Why did you take me on?'

She said 'Trade secret.'

We were quiet for a time. Everything seemed peaceful: in the world away from a theatre; in front of a fire; beyond the window.

I thought — Life is held in a riddle: like a universe; like an atom.

Then I thought — But I must tell you about my film!

She said 'Magic however depends on some talent. A fitting in. Perhaps a skill.'

I thought — As in my film?

She said 'You've had a pretty odd experience of life after all. Your father and mother are I suppose exceptional people. You've had to form yourself from them. Then you've been thrown into the world of your Uncle Bill and Mrs Washbourne. You've had a glimpse of this sort of power: some of it's fantasy and some of it's not. I mean there are some areas power touches and some it just doesn't. This has given you an exaggerated idea perhaps about the impossibility of organising things materially, except by some sort of casting of straws on the wind. But it's not all like this. I know some of it is. And perhaps you're right not to talk about this much. But I think you should realise that there are quite modest ways in which you can affect things for good or ill, quite practically; just by working at them; often, yes, in quite negative ways; that is, by correcting this or that abuse. Your Uncle Bill seems to have been quite good at this. You could learn from him in these ways probably. You may be right in your supposition that one cannot control the way things grow, but one can certainly deal with the needs that are preventing them.'

I said 'Yes.'

She said 'Now you've led me into one of your appalling horticultural metaphors.'

I said 'Like analysis.'

She said 'Like analysis.'

I said 'Dig away and — Abracadabra!'

She stirred in her seat restlessly.

I said 'Oh, and I met that girl again the other day.'

She said 'What girl?'

I said 'Judith Ponsonby.'

I thought — What has grown is not just that I have stopped feeling ashamed about not being interested in all those things I thought I should be interested in —

She said 'You still think the processes of analysis are mysterious?'

I said 'Aren't they?'

She said 'You used to talk to me about yourself as if I were not there.'

I thought — And now, it is unnerving, because I see you are?

I said 'If it's more than the exorcising of giants and dragons — is it something to do with making connections between the two sides of the brain?'

She said 'I don't know, is it?'

I thought — Like making love?

I said 'What does this friend of yours do, who's also the friend of my sister's?'

She said 'He's interested, yes, in biology and chemistry and physics; currently, in some study of the activity of the brain.'

XXVI

I thought — Now, my white bird, are we not pulling together well along this sea-shore?

One evening shortly before I was due to go to the university Uncle Bill came up to see me. He said —

'I've been in Manchester: Blackpool. What a life! It's a great game while you're at it. They want you for what they imagine; it doesn't matter what you tell them. I sometimes wonder if you couldn't get yourself stuffed and worked by one of those silicon chips, you know, they wouldn't know the difference.

'Three things I've wanted to do in politics, and I've done two of them. I've wanted to get on with this participation deal; and I've wanted to finish what we started with Perhaia. God knows there are going to be enough poor devils in Africa; not just ours; it was a tragedy about Perhaia. There'll come a time, soon enough, God knows, when if you've got a good man, you'll have to send out a dummy.

'You and I have had some good talks; haven't we; and I wouldn't like you to leave here with too low a regard for politics. It seems all a bit of a scramble every now and then; a safety match, you once called it. But we haven't really found a better way. If people don't bang on a bit, they kill each other. You once said I remember — But aren't things too dangerous now? But what would be more dangerous? You can't change things too much when the aeroplane's out of control. And you're in the driving seat. You might say — Well, are you? Or — Isn't that just the time when things change anyway? But things are more complicated now than when you just held — a joystick; a tiller.

'Mavis tells me you were pretty good the other day. I'm grateful. I've always tried to keep family life separate from public life; and I've succeeded. But I've sometimes wondered if it's been worth it. Nellie was always more of the public figure, you know. Mavis wanted to be an actress. Unlike your mother. Not much time for the humdrum stuff. A great girl, your mother! But someone's got to do it. I mean the humdrum stuff. Like politics. Mavis might have wanted to do a bit more of it later on; but by then it was difficult.

'Someone was telling me the other day of the casualties suffered by politicians' families: this is a fact, apparently. There are quite a number of breakdowns; suicides. It's the feeling of being in the public eye I suppose: something gets frozen. But they tell me with this new treatment Mavis will soon be better. We never had children of our own of course. She said you were a great help to her the other day. I've told her you'll see her.

'Nellie says you've managed to do quite a lot of work here; I'm glad. Of course, we'll be sorry to lose you. But you're right to go to a university. What are you reading?

'I think you've heard I'm resigning. For personal reasons. Quite personal reasons. If you hear anything to the contrary, I'd be glad if you'd say so.

'I don't think it would be accurate to say that I'm going to devote the rest of my life to family matters, though it's true I haven't spent enough time with Mavis. Who's Sextus Empiricus?'

Uncle Bill had picked up a book from beside my bed and was leafing through it.

I said 'He's a Sceptical philosopher of the third century AD.'

Uncle Bill said 'I've never heard of him.'

I said 'He said that one could never be certain of anything, but that uncertainty was necessary for mental health. People who thought they knew things for certain, were demented.'

Uncle Bill said 'Then Mavis isn't demented.'

I said 'What is her treatment?'

Uncle Bill put down the book and moved around the room.

I thought — He is like one of the boys that used to hang around my bed at school?

He said 'No shock. No violence. These new people. Wouldn't you agree?'

I said 'Yes.'

He said 'They seem to think, really, she just needs someone to make sense with her.'

I wondered — Are the people to whom Aunt Mavis has been sent, anything to do with Dr Anders?

Then Uncle Bill said 'I wish I'd had time for philosophy.'

I said 'I don't think I'll do philosophy.'

He said 'What will you do?'

I said 'Biology or chemistry or physics.'

He had come back to the table by my bed and was looking at a sort of model that I had made which consisted of a flat circular disc made of cardboard about five centimetres in diameter which could rotate round a central pin: at a point on the circumference there were attached two bits of elastic about eight centimetres long, one of which had its other end fastened to a pin somewhere below the disc, and the other had its other end free. The whole contraption was mounted on cardboard.

I said 'That's catastrophe theory.'

Uncle Bill said 'Catastrophe theory.'

I said 'It's a model to demonstrate a mathematical theory about how, in life, things work in sudden jumps, as opposed to how they work with simple matter which is smoothly. Now if you take hold of this free end of elastic here — '

I took hold of the free end of the elastic —

' — and stretch it, and move it in this space above the disc — '

I stretched the elastic and moved the free end smoothly in an area above the disc —

' — then the disc, held by the other bit of elastic, stays where it is for a time: then suddenly it jumps to a new position.'

The disc flicked round and seemed to hang there quivering.

I thought — Like a humming-bird?

I said 'It shows how, in life-sciences, pressure can build up steadily but either things do not change at all or else they change through what are called catastrophes — '

I was moving the free end of the elastic back in the space above the disc in order to make the disc jump to its former position when the pin in the middle suddenly flew out and the disc flopped on to the floor lethargically.

Uncle Bill said 'Never mind, that always happens.'

I said 'It explains things like how cells divide. Or how flowers open. Or how there are collapses on the Stock Exchange.'

Uncle Bill said 'That would be useful.'

I was trying to get the pin back through the hole in the disc and into the base again.

I said 'The point is, if it's working properly, one should be able to imagine what life is like a bit more clearly — '

He said 'Like Sextus Empiricus.'

I thought — Is that clever?

I said ' — and so stay healthy.'

I thought — That bird behind Uncle Bill's eyes after all has not died?

When I had mended my model, Uncle Bill played with it for a time delicately.

He said 'As a matter of fact, I've been offered a job at a university.'

I said 'Really?'

I thought — Not my university!

I said 'Are you going to take it?'

He said 'Ah, if I were younger — '

The disc flipped round. He watched it.

I thought — Put your hand on Aunt Mavis' forehead and say — Get it out, get it out —

He said 'There's this area above the disc in which when you move the end of the elastic the disc stays the same; then when you move it out of the area it flips.'

I said 'Yes, that's right.'

He said 'The interesting thing mathematically, would be, wouldn't it, the description of this area.'

I said 'Yes, that really is right!'

He left my model and walked round the room.

I wondered — But what on earth was it that made him for so long interested in things like politics, banging about inside his pin-table?

I said 'What shall I say to Aunt Mavis?'

He said 'She has this terrible sense of shame.'

I said 'But that's ridiculous!'

He said 'One of the points of a model would be, wouldn't it, that you often can't talk directly about life, but you can demonstrate how things work, and so help things change for the better.'

I said 'I'll tell her that.'

He said 'Ah, you're no Sceptic!'

I thought — What is that other image that has been coming into my mind recently: that of a grub that hibernates through a long summer and then bursts out into a butterfly —

Uncle Bill said 'You should talk to a friend of mine.'

I said 'Who?'

He said 'He writes plays.'

I thought — I'm not jealous?

Then — That is another example of catastrophe: when an insect, or a person, starts to become an imago —

Uncle Bill said 'What his plays are about, if I understand them, is that old forms of dramatics are cracking up; and some new sort of head is emerging.'

XXVII

I thought — O world outside, are there any other signs of life in this experiment?

I had a letter from Tammy Burns. It said —

Dear Bert,

It was good to hear from you. I'm just off on a walking trip along the Great Wall of China. But I'd like to send you, through my agent, some cinematic equipment I've recently ordered, but now have no use for. This consists of a 1237XL Bell and Howell camera, and a Sankyo 700 projector with f1.4 lens. I'm not sure if this will quite do what you have in mind, but it will be a start anyway. I look forward to seeing you when I get back.

I tried to call on you the other day, but there seemed to be quite a crowd outside the stage door.

Take care.

> Best
> Tammy

I thought — Imago: Im-a-go: how do you pronounce it?

Once during these days before I went to the university I went to see Sheila and Brian Alick. They now lived openly together in Sheila's room. Brian had moved the squatters out of the house; the bedsprings were raised respectably on wooden blocks.

Brian Alick sat with his arm round Sheila. They looked as if they were about to be photographed for a Sunday newspaper.

Brian Alick said —

'I'm not saying it was deliberate, no. I'm not saying that. But in fifteen years of political work the one time I've thrown over political principles for personal considerations has been, well — I'm not saying this against you Bert. I'm satisfied it was not.

It's significant, though, that the one time one has found oneself in a position of — I won't say obligation — I'm saying there are two fundamental attitudes: two quite different basic options: and you've got to choose: you can't mix oil and water: if you think you can, then God watch out!'

Sheila said 'Nowadays they simply have you committed, you know?'

I wanted to ask — Whatever happened to that man in white overalls?

I said 'Well, I'm glad it's turned out all right.'

Brian Alick said 'It hasn't turned out all right!'

Sheila said 'It hasn't turned out all right at all!'

I thought — And in this room I once hung in my small nest that was like a breast.

I went round to see Sally Rogers.

Sally said —

'But the whole thing's coming out inch by inch, you know. What a salmagundi! If it wasn't just so, you'd have to invent it. Nellie Washbourne had this husband, people didn't know about. They were in the Lebanon in the nineteen-fifties. Well, he turned up the other day; or someone did: and God knows what they'd got on Nellie! There are supposed to be some photographs. This was just at the time of that party for Perhaia. No wonder Nellie got the wind up! And fell into the fire. And there was a shot: do you know about a shot? by a security man; someone trying to break in; through a window; to get at Nellie. I suppose your uncle just wanted to scare them off.'

I thought — I will try to make love properly with Sally Rogers.

She did not seem to want to at first. She said 'You'll be looking down your nose at me.'

I said 'What else might you want me to do with it?'

Then some time in the middle of the night when we were lying side by side in the dark Sally said 'What are you thinking?'

I said 'What was the name of Mrs Washbourne's husband?'

She said 'I suppose, Washbourne.'

Then in the morning she said 'You won't leave for a day or two, will you?'

One day I rang up Judith Ponsonby. I thought — Remember, remember — like Guy Fawkes, or St Augustine, was it? — you may want the pain some time, but not now.

'Judith?'

'Yes?'

'This is Bert.'

'Oh Bert!'

That voice like boiling oil; like tinkling cymbals.

'I wondered if I could see you.'

'Oh Bert, I'd adore to, but I'm going away today.'

'Where are you going?'

'To Jerusalem.'

I thought, for some reason — Well that's all right.

I said 'I want to return your five-pound note.'

She said 'Keep it for me, will you, till I get back.'

I said 'Yes.'

She said 'I hear you're going to a university.'

I said 'How did you hear that?'

'Ah, I have my spies you see!'

I said 'Why don't you come too?'

'Perhaps I will.'

Then I said — 'I'm wondering what I can do to make you want to see me now.'

I thought — I'm doing this wrong: or am I?

— In order to see what happens, I say what is true —

She said 'But promise, promise, to see me when I get back.'

'I said "I promise" — '

She said 'You do?'

I said ' — is not being true.'

I thought — Can I now spend the five-pound note?

Then when I was walking through streets again I thought — But I am happy: I am happy! You do not get to Shakespeare's recognition scenes except through forests and over mountains —

One day I rang up my sister. I said —

'How's the baby?'

'Very well thank you.'

'I want to see it being born.'

184

'Of course you can't see it being born!'
I said 'Why not?' Then — 'How are the fathers?'
'Very well thank you.'
I said 'Well, aren't I sort of its father too?'
— In these imagining days; floating slightly above roof-
tops —
She said 'Anyway, he says he's met you.'
'Who?'
'The father.'
I thought — Oh God, and just when I was thinking I was
getting a bit of immunity —
I said 'Where?'
She said 'At some sort of reception. Of Uncle Bill's.'
I thought — Oh but I knew! I knew!
She said 'You don't seem very interested.'
I said 'Oh but I am!'
She said 'He seemed to think you were very nice.'
I said 'Well I seemed to think he was very nice too.'
I stood with my head against the glass wall of a call box.
There seemed to be fingers tapping and clinking to get in from
outside.
I said 'I mean, it's just that it's difficult — '
She said 'What's difficult?'
I thought I might say — This recognition scene.
I said 'Tall, with spectacles.'
She said 'Yes.' Then — 'He writes plays.'
How could I explain — This happiness —
Then I thought — Will the baby be able to bear it? This
break-up of our old genes; the head like a butterfly emerging
from what we have made of ourselves, from our fathers and our
mothers —
My sister said 'And how's Aunt Mavis?'
I said 'She's better.'
'Is she in a home?'
'No.'
I thought — All these miracles.
My sister said 'Well, will you be its godfather then?'
I said 'Yes!'

I thought — My life will be with these people then.

There was a day when I was standing in one of my favourite places by the river and I was watching the water going past to the sea and a wind was blowing and I thought I could go in any way that I liked since life was like a flower from which I could pluck off the petals — She loves me, she loves me not — and what I was talking to was not now myself but life; and by counting the petals I could ensure that the petal I wanted was the one carried by the wind — She loves me — and by turning this way or that I could determine which way the wind came in since life was also inside me; and then the petal I had chosen might return in future days as the bird or imago with the petal in its mouth.